Sadie

The Amish of Morrissey County Book One

Sylvia Price

Penn and Ink Writing, LLC

Stay Up to Date with Sylvia Price

Subscribe to Sylvia's newsletter at newsletter.sylviaprice.com to get to know Sylvia and her family. It's also a great way to stay in the loop about new releases, freebies, promos, and more.

As a thank-you, you will receive several FREE exclusive short stories that aren't available for purchase.

HOPE
for Hannah's
LOVE
Amish Love Through the Seasons
SYLVIA PRICE

SYLVIA PRICE
EVE
AN ELIJAH COMPANION STORY

Praise for Sylvia Price's Books

“Author Sylvia Price wrote a storyline that enthralled me. The characters are unique in their own way, which made it more interesting. I highly recommend reading this book. I'll be reading more of Author Sylvia Price's books.”

“You can see the love of the main characters and the love that the author has for the main characters and her writing. This book is so wonderful. I cannot wait to read more from this beautiful writer.”

“The storyline caught my attention from the very beginning and kept me interested throughout the entire book. I loved the chemistry between the characters.”

“A wonderful, sweet and clean story with strong characters. Now I just need to know what happens next!”

“First time reading this author, and I’m very impressed! I love feeling the godliness of this story.”

“This was a wonderful story that reminded me of a glorious God we have.”

“I encourage all to read this uplifting story of faith and friendship.”

“I love Sylvia's books because they are filled with love and faith.”

Other Books by Sylvia Price

Jonah's Redemption: Book 1 – FREE
Jonah's Redemption: Book 2 – http://getbook.at/jonah2
Jonah's Redemption: Book 3 – http://getbook.at/jonah3
Jonah's Redemption: Book 4 – http://getbook.at/jonah4
Jonah's Redemption: Book 5 – http://getbook.at/jonah5
Jonah's Redemption: Boxed Set – http://getbook.at/jonahset

The Christmas Arrival – http://getbook.at/christmasarrival
Seeds of Spring Love (Amish Love Through the Seasons Book 1) – http://getbook.at/seedsofspring
Sprouts of Summer Love (Amish Love Through the Seasons Book 2) – http://getbook.at/

sproutsofsummer

Fruits of Fall Love (Amish Love Through the Seasons Book 3) – http://getbook.at/fruitsoffall

Waiting for Winter Love (Amish Love Through the Seasons Book 4) – http://getbook.at/waitingforwinter

Amish Love Through the Seasons Boxed Set (The Complete Series) – http://getbook.at/amishseasons

Elijah: An Amish Story of Crime and Romance – http://getbook.at/elijah

The Christmas Cards – http://getbook.at/christmascards

A Promised Tomorrow (The Yoder Family Saga Prequel) – FREE

Peace for Yesterday (The Yoder Family Saga Book 1) – http://getbook.at/peaceforyesterday

A Path for Tomorrow (The Yoder Family Saga Book 2) – http://getbook.at/pathfortomorrow

Faith for the Future (The Yoder Family Saga Book 3) – http://getbook.at/faithforthefuture

Patience for the Present (The Yoder Family Saga Book 4) – http://getbook.at/patienceforthepresent

Return to Yesterday (The Yoder Family Saga Book 5) – http://getbook.at/returntoyesterday
The Yoder Family Saga Boxed Set (The Complete Series) – http://getbook.at/yoderbox

The Origins of Cardinal Hill (The Amish of Cardinal Hill Prequel) – FREE
The Beekeeper's Calendar (The Amish of Cardinal Hill Book 1) – http://getbook.at/beekeeperscalendar
The Soapmaker's Recipe (The Amish of Cardinal Hill Book 2) – http://getbook.at/soapmakersrecipe
The Herbalist's Remedy (The Amish of Cardinal Hill Book 3) – http://getbook.at/herbalistsremedy

Sarah (The Amish of Morrissey County Prequel) – FREE
Sadie (The Amish of Morrissey County Book 1) – http://getbook.at/sadie
Bridget (The Amish of Morrissey County Book 2) – http://getbook.at/bridget
Abigail (The Amish of Morrissey County Book 3) – http://getbook.at/morrisseyabigail
Eliza (The Amish of Morrissey County Book 4) – http://getbook.at/eliza
Dorothy (The Amish of Morrissey County

Book 5) – http://getbook.at/dorothy

Songbird Cottage Beginnings (Pleasant Bay Prequel) – FREE

The Songbird Cottage (Pleasant Bay Book 1) – http://getbook.at/songbirdcottage

Return to Songbird Cottage (Pleasant Bay Book 2) – http://getbook.at/returntosongbird

Escape to Songbird Cottage (Pleasant Bay Book 3) – http://getbook.at/escapetosongbird

Secrets of Songbird Cottage (Pleasant Bay Book 4) – http://getbook.at/secretsofsongbird

Seasons at Songbird Cottage (Pleasant Bay Book 5) – http://getbook.at/seasonsatsongbird

The Songbird Cottage Boxed Set (Pleasant Bay Complete Series Collection) – http://getbook.at/songbirdbox

The Crystal Crescent Inn (Sambro Lighthouse Book 1) – http://getbook.at/cci1

The Crystal Crescent Inn (Sambro Lighthouse Book 2) – http://getbook.at/cci2

The Crystal Crescent Inn (Sambro Lighthouse Book 3) – http://getbook.at/cci3

The Crystal Crescent Inn (Sambro Lighthouse Book 4) – http://getbook.at/cci4

The Crystal Crescent Inn (Sambro Lighthouse Book 5) – http://getbook.at/cci5

The Crystal Crescent Inn Boxed Set (Sambro Lighthouse Complete Series Collection) – http://getbook.at/ccibox

Contents

Unofficial Glossary of Pennsylvania Dutch Words

Ach – Oh
Amisch – Amish
Bruder/brieder – brother(s)
Bu – boy
Daed – dad
Danki – thanks
Dochder – daughter
Eldre – parents
Englisch/Englischer – non-Amish person
Familye – family
Fraa – wife
Gmay – local Amish community
Gott – God
Groossdaadi – grandfather
Groosseldre – grandparents
Groossmammi – grandmother
Gude daag – Hello (literally Good day)

Gut – good

Kapp – Amish head covering

Kind/Kinner – child/children

Kinnskind/Kinnskinner – grandchild(ren)

Kumm – come

Liewi – dear

Maedel/maed – girl(s)

Maem – mom

Mann/Menner – husband(s)/man

Nee – no

Rumspringa – running around period for Amish youth

Schweigersoh – son-in-law

Schweschder/schweschdre – sister(s)

Sing – a Sunday evening social gathering of Amish youth

Wunderbaar – wonderful

Ya – yes

Chapter One

1991

Morrissey County, Pennsylvania

The library. Ever since Sadie Renno was just a little child, the large brick library seemed to woo her. Raised in the Amish faith, she had no television or phone for recreation—books were therefore her only source of entertainment, and Sadie relished them.

Visits to the library were always what Sadie looked forward to most, and that afternoon, she had been thrilled when her Aunt Bethany offered to take her. Her heart skipped in anticipation as she made her way up the steps that led to the front doors.

While Sadie was always diligently careful not to browse any books that were forbidden by her Amish community; the library was her opportunity to break free from the monotony of everyday life. Within its walls were stories about pioneers and settlers braving the new world and taming the wild frontier, of pirates that long ago sailed the seas, and of mysteries waiting to be explored and uncovered.

While the Amish lifestyle offered Sadie a relatively boring existence and one that consisted of the same events day after day, the library opened her mind to an entirely new world.

"I'll be over there looking for the next book in the pioneer series I'm reading," Aunt Bethany had told her as she gave Sadie an affectionate pat on the back, giving her the freedom to go explore the rest of the library at will.

Meandering through the aisles of books, ten-year-old Sadie inhaled deeply the scent of ink on pages and closed her eyes in bliss. There was something about the smell of books that drew her in, captivating her senses and compelling her to start reading.

Don't look at the magazine section. Her father's voice echoed in Sadie's ears even though he'd never gone to the library with her. Her father was always anxious to offer suggestions and advice that would keep her from falling prey to the wild side of life.

Glancing toward her aunt, who was busy

looking in the Christian romance section, Sadie bit down on her lip. Determined to obey her father, she walked past the magazine display with her gaze fixed resolutely ahead as she made her way to the young adult section.

If her father knew what some of the books in that area contained, Sadie was almost certain that he would forbid her from looking at them as well. Thankfully, Jacob Renno wasn't one to keep up with novels.

Walking past one of the study tables that were set up in the middle of the library, Sadie stopped dead in her tracks. There, sitting on the table, was a pile of horse magazines.

Glancing around furtively to make sure that her aunt wasn't watching, Sadie lowered herself into one of the chairs and tentatively reached for a magazine. What could it hurt, after all? Wasn't her father being a little paranoid to forbid her from looking at what was technically just a picture book of horses?

Flipping the magazine open, the soft pages tickled her fingertips, and she breathed out a sigh of awe as she looked at the pictures displayed before her. A large black barn silhouetted by a brilliant sunset stared back at her. Looking closer, she spied a woman in a pair of blue jeans getting into a truck that was pulling a horse trailer behind it. The entire image mesmerized her. There was something about it that drew her in, filling her with a yearning to be a part of the scene.

As her gaze dropped down to her own plain blue dress, Sadie's heart followed suit and plummeted. She didn't want to be a simple, boring Amish girl with no future outside of her traditional community. Glancing back at the picture, she imagined how nice it would be to be the woman climbing up into the truck. Carefree and independent, she certainly looked like she had a goal and a purpose for her life. And happiness. Contentment.

At only the tender age of ten, Sadie already sometimes questioned whether happiness was a fundamental part of her life. Scrunching her face into a frown, she considered all the times that her father had warned her against the *Englisch* lifestyle. He made it sound like everyone outside of their faith was depraved and told her that the modern world was filled with nothing but sugar-coated troubles and heartaches.

As she drank in the pictures of the magazine, it was truly hard for Sadie to believe that he was right. What she was seeing was a lifestyle that looked inviting, pure, and free. Wouldn't that be so much better than what the Amish had to offer?

"What if they're all just pretending that the world is dangerous?" Sadie whispered to herself as she turned a page in the magazine to reveal another beautiful picture. "What if my *daed* and all the *gmay* leaders are simply lying to us to make us stay *Amisch*?"

What if, rather than protecting her, her father was simply trying to control her?

Her aunt's voice as she talked to someone startled Sadie from her tangential thoughts, and she looked up just in time to see her aunt checking out the books that she had picked out in the Christian romance section. Heart thumping in her chest, Sadie hurried to close the magazine and set it back in its place. She hadn't been caught, and she certainly had no intention of admitting that she had been looking at forbidden magazines; yet, something indeterminable felt distinctly different as she walked away from them.

In that moment, it became crystal clear to Sadie that she wanted a life outside of her grasp. And no matter what, she determined that she was going to do whatever it took to get that life. Even if it cost her everything.

Chapter Two

Eight Years Later

Though it was a beautiful spring day with a cloudless sky, Sadie felt like the weight of the world pressed on her chest. A lonely sadness spread through her as she stood beside her mother's grave. Although it was untraditional for the Amish to visit the graves of their relatives and her father and grandfather would never think of visiting Sarah Renno's grave, Sadie felt closer to the mother she never knew when she went to the cemetery. Her father's stories of how he had met her mother when she was lamenting at her grandmother's grave gave Sadie even more of a desire to break with convention and walk in her mother's shoes.

"I wish you were still here with me, *Maem*," Sadie whispered as she reached up to wipe a tear from her cheek. "I wish I'd had the chance to know you...but you were ripped away from me before I could even see your face." She mindlessly watched a bird hopping across the grass and looking for a worm as she nibbled her lip in thought. Sucking in a fortifying deep breath, she stood up straighter and said, "I know people think that little *kinner* are the ones who need their *maems* the most...but I'm convinced that I need you more now than I ever did when I was a *kind*."

Sadie closed her eyes and squeezed them tightly shut in a bid to collect her emotions, but tears rebelliously forced their way past her eyelids.

"Being *Amisch* is so very difficult," she enunciated between gritted teeth—as if the gravestone could actually hear and understand her. "I heard that you had struggles in the *gmay* too. How I wish that you were here to be a sounding board, to be a listening ear for all my questions and doubts, and to give me sage advice. Perhaps I wouldn't hate being *Amisch* so much if you were here for me."

Ever since Sadie was a toddler, her father had assured her that the Lord had a good plan when He took Sarah Renno home to heaven so early in life. Just the thought made Sadie grimace all over again. Did that mean that God was behind the pain and suffering in life? Sometimes, Sadie found herself wondering if He existed at all. Surely, it was senseless that a good Creator would put them through so much. Why would He give her life, only to rip her mother away when she was born?

Regarding the gravestone while deep in thought, Sadie wondered if her mother ever actually overcame her desire for the *Englisch* lifestyle or if she had simply learned to suppress it. These were the questions that Sadie needed to ask but would never have opportunity to do so.

Sadie had just turned eighteen years old. Curling the side of her lip under her teeth, she considered all that might mean to her life. Her grandfather, Bishop Kauffman, was already bearing down hard, trying to convince her that it was time for her to get baptized into the Amish faith. Many of her friends were already signing up for baptismal classes, taking the first step toward signing their lives away to staying Amish.

"But I don't want to be *Amisch*," she spoke aloud into the spring air as she reached up to push a strand of loose hair away from her face and back under her prayer *kapp*.

Sadie closed her eyes and let her mind travel back to the long-ago image that she had seen in a horse magazine when she was still basically a child: the woman in blue jeans, hair pulled back in a ponytail, leading a horse and smiling from ear-to-ear. It had been a picture that made Sadie wish she were part of the scene.

She still wished she were part of that scene.

"I'm sorry, *Maem*," Sadie managed to choke out around a sob. "I don't know how you would feel about it, but I have no intention at all of staying *Amisch*. I just can't do it. As soon as I can possibly gather up the courage, I'm going to leave this place. I'm going to chase my dreams of something better. All I'm doing right now is biding my time until I find my opportunity."

Setting a bouquet of wildflowers down on the gravesite, which she had picked from the local flowering flora on the way to the cemetery, Sadie stepped back to regard it. Wiping her eyes, she attempted to stave off the overwhelming myriad emotions; it wouldn't do to return home to her father in tears. He would then surely know that something was wrong. Squaring her shoulders, she stood straighter and took in a deep breath of air. It was time to head home. She had said her goodbyes to her mother. Now she was just going to bide her time, waiting and watching for her chance to break away from her strict Amish lifestyle.

Making the short trip home on foot, Sadie soaked in the warmth of the morning and the sound of birds singing in the trees overhead. As she walked by an *Englisch* neighbor's house, she gazed into their yard, where she saw three children bouncing up and down on a trampoline. Through the open window, she could see a mother watching television as she cooked. A car pulled into the drive, and the father got out.

It seemed like such a beautiful picture yet so far out of Sadie's reach. How could she ever hope to become *Englisch*? She had no money and no connections to the *Englisch* life. To break free from the Amish and truly become a normal person, she would have to find a way to get a driver's license, get a vehicle, find a job, and find a place to live—all without a birth certificate or Social Security card.

Frowning to herself, Sadie shook her head. She was determined to find some way to do it—even if she had to start out living under a bridge. Her father wasn't going to be able to force her to stay Amish for the rest of her life. Sadie was going to make sure of that!

Chapter Three

Aaron Miller reached to pull the pitcher of milk out of the icebox in his family's kitchen. The echoes of two of his younger brothers bickering over who had won a game of checkers drifted into the kitchen. Chuckling to himself, Aaron listened as his mother threatened to spank them both—even if it was Sunday—if they didn't stop their squabbling.

As the third of seven children in the Miller family, Aaron was no stranger to disputes and disagreements. While his siblings generally got along well, the occasional discord was what his mother claimed was the cause of her graying hair.

"*Ach*!" Becky Miller exclaimed as she walked into the kitchen with a triumphant grin on her face. "I tell you, you *kinner* might just be the death of me."

Putting up his hands to indicate his innocence,

Aaron laughed and said, "Don't look at me. I've never caused you any problems, have I, *Maem*?"

Walking to his side, Becky gave her son a pat on the back and shook her head with a chuckle. "Of all my *kinner*, I have to say you are the one who has given me the least amount of trouble."

Bending over, Aaron gave his mother a kiss on the cheek. While he had been joking with his question, he also knew that he had been a relatively easy-to-manage boy. Aaron had always had a pleasant, contented way about him. He had always known what he wanted out of life and had always been convinced that he was exactly where God had planted him.

Stephan Miller swung the door open and stepped into the kitchen, a wide grin on his face. Aaron's father's cheerful attitude always made him seem younger than his actual years.

"I was out checking on the cows and just had a yearning for some of your homemade chocolate chip cookies!" Stephan announced with a twinkle in his eye.

Putting a hand on her hip, Becky raised an eyebrow and said, "Today is Sunday. Have you forgotten I don't usually cook on Sundays?" Smirking the tiniest bit, she added, "But you're in luck. I happened to bake some last night." Reaching up and rummaging in a cabinet, she pulled down a covered plate and pushed aside the top to reveal an arrangement of cookies.

Watching as his father stepped forward to dig into the offered cookies, Aaron couldn't help but smile to himself. Observing his parents interacting had always been such a pleasure to him. They had such a rapport between them.

Aaron could only hope that one day he would be able to find a girl who would regard him with the same love and respect which his mother bestowed upon his father. They had a solid relationship built on trust and years of working side by side.

While his parents filled very traditional roles in the Amish community, they always made sure that they were a team. Stephan was always tinkering with some carpentry project, while Becky helped to support the family by not only tending to the house but also doing sewing for *Englisch* neighbors and friends.

Snagging a cookie of his own, Aaron said, "*Ach*, I sure am glad you thought to make these last night, *Maem*! This is just what I need to tide me over on my way to the *sing*."

His parents exchanged teasing glances with each other, and Stephan said, "I hope you manage to find yourself a *maedel* who will bake you cookies so you won't steal so many of these. But I know they'll never beat your *maem's*."

Becky jabbed her husband playfully in the side, her face growing red as she said, "Goodness, Stephan! You already married me—no need to lay on the compliments so thick!"

Snaking his arm around his wife, Stephan pulled her close and chuckled as he replied, "But that, *Liewi*, is how I get more cookies!"

Glancing at the clock, Aaron realized how late it was getting. It was already five o'clock in the evening, and the young folk would soon be gathering at Ned Schmidt's home for their weekly *sing*.

Bidding his parents goodbye, he hurried out the door and toward the barn. Aaron always enjoyed the young peoples' gatherings. It was enjoyable to get to see the other teenagers while playing games with them and having fun. But now Aaron had a new reason to enjoy going to the *sings*.

Sadie Renno.

The mere thought of her name induced a smile on his lips. He wasn't sure when the young woman had caught his eye, but it seemed like she was all he thought about now when he considered attending the *sings*.

Shaking his head and chuckling to himself, he hurried on out to hitch up the buggy. He was going to have to get his mind out of the cloud and focus on getting ready, or he wouldn't make it to the *sing* in time to see Sadie at all

∞∞∞

Standing in front of the mirror in her bedroom, Sadie worked to push some of her blonde hair back under her prayer *kapp*. Grabbing a bottle of scented lotion, she squirted some on her hands and then rubbed it into her skin.

"Well, here we go again," she muttered to her reflection. "Another *sing* to endure."

Sadie hadn't always hated going to the *sings*. When she first turned sixteen, it had actually been a fun escape to get out with the other young folk and enjoy spending time away from her father. But as time had gone by and more of Sadie's friends started to pair off with boys, the more uncomfortable the gatherings had become.

Now everyone her age wanted to chat about their boyfriends and marriage.

Shaking her head, Sadie tried to keep her stomach from flopping. She almost hated going to the *sings* now.

Sadie groaned when, as she made her way downstairs, she saw Grandfather Kauffman sitting with her father near the fireplace. The two men were talking, yet Sadie knew why her grandfather was there—he had come over from his nearby farm to give her a ride to the *sing*.

Sometimes, it felt like her family was convinced that they needed to completely hold her hostage in the community, not allowing her a moment's respite out of their sight.

"*Daed*." Sadie started toward his chair with a frown on her face. She could only hope that she would get his sympathy. "I'm not feeling well tonight. I think I'll just skip the *sing* and go next week."

Raising an eyebrow, Jacob Renno stared at her with concern etched on his face. "Sadie, this is the second Sunday in a row that you've complained of feeling bad."

"How do you expect to ever find a suitable *Amisch* beau if you don't go to the *sings*?" Bishop

Kauffman spoke up as he struck the end of his cane against the floor. "Our entire lifestyle is based around the *familye* unit. If you don't go out and find an *Amisch bu* to court you, how will you ever expect to fit in with our *gmay*?"

It took all that Sadie possessed to keep from rolling her eyes right at her grandfather. She loved and respected the older man, but sometimes he aggravated her to no end.

Squaring her shoulders, she straightened herself and announced, "Then I guess I'm ready to go." Surely, it would be better to just go to the *sing* rather than risk one of her grandfather's long lectures.

Like it or not, it appeared that Sadie would be gathering with the Amish young folk again. And, knowing the way things went, she would probably be going every Sunday night until she was finally free from the slow suffocation by the boa constrictor of the Amish life.

∞∞∞

Mingling with a group of the Amish young men, Aaron tried to at least appear like he was listening to what they were saying. Nearby, some of the young folk had gotten together and were bumping a volleyball back and forth over the top of a net. While they hadn't started an official game yet, they were clearly warming up.

There, in the midst of all the young folk, was Sadie Renno.

Just watching her, Aaron found himself becoming tongue-tied and dry-mouthed. A part of him wanted to go over and talk to her, while another part of him felt like he was so uncomfortable he would surely fall flat on his face if he so much as tried to walk toward her. Aaron was totally captivated by her beauty as she unknowingly ran this way and that, trying to bump the ball back over the net.

Sadie was truly one of the prettiest girls in Morrissey with her flawless complexion and blonde hair. Her blue eyes matched a clear autumn sky, and her chin rounded to just the finest shape.

As Sadie played volleyball with her friends, Aaron found fragments of the Song of Solomon playing through his mind. Surely, this was the way that Solomon had been feeling when he penned the love book of the Bible.

"How amazing that *Gott* made something so

beautiful!" Aaron whispered to himself. Out of all things created in the world, woman had to be the most amazing. Allowing his mind to travel back to his mother, Aaron considered the ways that she almost single-handedly ran the entire household, took care of him and his siblings, and also helped to cover some of the bills with her sewing—all while providing emotional support to his father.

Looking at Sadie, he wondered if she would possibly be the help meant for him that had been described in the Bible—a woman who could come alongside him and partner with him, the two of them working together to do the Lord's will on earth.

"Seems like someone has a staring problem!" Joe Yoder giggled as he approached Aaron.

Aaron's face and neck flushed crimson as he realized he'd been caught so obviously staring. He took a step back and looked down at the ground. "*Ach*," he managed to mutter, "it's just a *gut* day to be looking around and do some people-watching..."

"*Ya*," Joe returned, reaching out to give Aaron a slap on the arm, "a *gut* day for woman-hunting you mean, and it looks like you have one in your sights!" Giving Aaron a nudge, he suggested, "The warm-up's done. Why don't you go talk to her?"

"I don't know..." Nervousness spread through Aaron's veins and permeated his being, almost overwhelming him. While he had conversations with girls from time to time, he wasn't exactly proficient or at ease doing it. The possibility of Sadie turning him down may as well have been a ten-ton weight shackled to each limb, rooting him to the spot.

"Listen, Aaron." Joe raised an eyebrow and gave him a knowing look as if he were much older and wiser. "If you don't try, you'll never catch her! Now get over there!"

The weights became unshackled at Joe's bolstering of Aaron's confidence, and he gave a determined nod and started in Sadie's direction.

The volleyball warm-up had ended, and the teenagers were now talking in little groups. Sadie had stepped back from the rest to fan her face under a nearby tree.

"*Gude daag*!" Aaron said as he stepped up to Sadie's side, grinning awkwardly. "You're Sadie, aren't you?"

Assessing him with disdain as if he'd just lost his mind, Sadie nodded and confirmed, "*Ya*, I am. I'm pretty sure you should know that by now. You might be a few years older than me, but we've lived in the same *gmay* our entire lives."

Sadie's stating the obvious only exacerbated Aaron's blush all the more. Casting his gaze down to his black boots, he stammered, "Uh-um...yes, well...I suppose..."

He was blowing it, and Aaron knew it! Surely, Sadie would now be convinced that he was out of his mind! A madman. He had to fight the urge not to turn and flee in the opposite direction. To say something so asinine to the girl that he had admired for so long seemed like something that could never be salvaged. He desperately racked his brain to try and steer the conversation into a less idiotic direction.

"Do you like playing volleyball?" Aaron asked, instantly wincing as he realized how stupid the question sounded.

Shrugging, Sadie replied, "I guess so. It's better than anything else I can think of doing."

"Game time, everyone!" The voice of Joe Yoder spoke above the crowd, "My team on this side, Pete Schwartz's team on the other!" He called out, "I want Aaron Miller on my team!"

While Aaron wasn't particularly skilled at playing volleyball, he was relieved to have a reason to make an escape from his humiliating dialogue. As much as he wanted to spend time with Sadie, he had made such a fool of himself that he felt like the only sane option was to recoup and try again later.

"I'll have Jonas Hill on mine!" Pete called out.

Looking pointedly at Aaron, Joe grinned and declared, "I'll have Sadie Renno on mine."

The rest of the names became a blur in Aaron's mind as Sadie stood up straighter and followed him over to Joe's side of the net. While Aaron appreciated his friend's attempts at pairing him with the pretty girl, he couldn't help but wish that Joe had left him well-enough alone. He had already been embarrassed enough for one night, and he feared that he might make a bigger fool of himself if he spent any more time around her!

Chapter Four

Sadie found herself feeling almost sorry for the slightly older Aaron Miller. While she and Aaron had never been friends, she had known him pretty well for most of her life. Glancing over at him as he stood at her side, Sadie had to admit that Aaron was quite good-looking. Working with his father in carpentry, he was not only tall but had also grown very muscular. He had a head full of curly dark hair and green eyes that practically sparkled.

Even more importantly, Aaron was a good man. He was known in the *gmay* for being kind-hearted, compassionate, and tender. He was honest to a fault and faithful to the point that others might feel put to shame. And above all, he was devoted to his faith.

"He's *too* faithful," Sadie mused to herself with a sad sigh.

Any germinating feelings she might have for Aaron needed to be nipped in the bud quickly. No matter how nice or attractive he might be, he was completely devoted to the Amish community and faith. He had joined the church two years prior, and Sadie knew that he was not the type to renege on his decision.

With Sadie's attraction to the *Englisch* world and outright plans to leave the Amish faith, it would do her no good to get attached to someone within the faith community. A relationship with Aaron would simply complicate the process while possibly breaking his heart.

Sadie squinted her eyes and tried to focus on the volleyball that was being held by the server on the opposing team. Suddenly, it came flying over the net, straight toward her. Sadie swung her arms and hit it, sending it back over to the other team.

Back and forth, back and forth, the ball went. When it came flying back, Aaron reached for it but stumbled and nearly missed. Another Amish youth managed to step up just in time to bump the ball back over the net to win the point.

Sadie couldn't help but find that her eyes were more drawn to Aaron than the ball, and he seemed to be having the same problem! Frowning, she tried to direct her attention on the game at hand. The ball came flying toward her again, and she stepped forward to hit it, only to slip. Just as she headed in a tumble to the ground, Aaron reached out an arm to break her fall. Helping her to her feet, they both laughed awkwardly as the game continued on around them.

"Are you all right?" Aaron asked as Sadie dusted some grass off her skirt.

Sadie nodded, and Joe called out, "Hey! I wanted you all to *play* on my team. I didn't choose you so you could *flirt*!"

Sadie's flushed face grew even warmer at the boy's insinuation. Pulling away from Aaron, she turned back to the game.

Sadie felt completely out of sorts. All of her attempts to keep the ball in the air seemed futile, and she made more mistakes than anything else. Aaron, too, seemed to be playing poorly.

When the game finally came to an end, the opposing team were the winners. Sadie was self-conscious and out of breath, exhausted both from the long game and her sorry attempts at playing well. Walking away from the rest of the teenagers, she lowered herself down to sit under a tree and leaned her head back against it as she tried to catch her breath. Closing her eyes, she found herself pondering the possibility of leaving the Amish and what exactly it might take to make it a reality.

"Thirsty?" A man's voice elicited a look of surprise from Sadie.

Aaron was standing over her, a bottle of water extended toward her while he held his own water in his other hand. Smiling sweetly, she nodded gratefully. There was something nice about his attempts to be friendly—even if she didn't feel the same way about him.

Reaching for the bottle, Sadie smiled and said, "*Danki*. I guess that did wear me out a little bit!"

To her absolute astonishment, Aaron lowered himself to the ground next to her. As she took a drink of her water, Sadie glanced at him out of the corner of her eye. He looked terribly awkward and uncomfortable.

Deciding that she would simply lay things out in an honest way for him, Sadie announced, "I didn't want to *kumm* tonight, but my *groossdaadi* and *daed* made me."

Her words had obviously gotten Aaron's attention. He raised his eyebrows in surprise and turned to look at her with shock written all over his face.

"Don't you enjoy the *sings*?"

Crossing her ankles, Sadie lifted her water bottle to her lips and took a sip. Staring at the other young folk that were still playing, she wished that Aaron would set his sights on one of them. Surely, one of the other girls would be more his type and more interested in his sort of lifestyle.

"*Nee*," Sadie replied with a shake of her head as she set her water bottle aside. "Honestly, I don't find much about *sings* fun anymore. Or the *Amisch* lifestyle at all, actually." Sucking in a deep breath, she let it out slowly as she said, "I don't really know that the *Amisch* life is for me."

Glancing over at Aaron, she could see that he was stunned by her declaration. He opened his mouth and then shut it, seemingly contemplating her words before finally saying, "Surely, you don't feel that way. You must just be having a bad weekend."

Sadie snorted at his naïveté. He knew nothing about her, yet he was already anxious to try to force her to follow his path—just like her father and grandfather.

Turning to look straight at him, Sadie firmly replied, "Aaron, if it were possible, I would leave the *Amisch* right now." Motioning toward the other young folk, she tried to explain, "I don't fit here. Can't you see that?"

As soon as the words escaped her lips, Sadie realized in horror that tears were beginning to gather at the corners of her eyes. She had never talked to anyone other than her mother's gravestone about her desire to leave the Amish faith. Now that she had opened her heart to Aaron, she realized that the pain might be more than she could bear.

"Sadie." Aaron paused, seemingly weighing his words before speaking. Finally, he took a deep breath and said, "I just think that if you were to actually experience the real world, you might not find the *Englisch* so attractive either. I think we have things pretty *gut*. We lead nice, peaceful, quiet lives."

Sadie was tempted to snap back with a retort but chose to hold her tongue. Aaron was right; she didn't know much about the *Englisch*, but he didn't either. Who was he to try to lecture her? It seemed that everyone she talked to about anything just wanted to judge her and force her into the box they had planned for her. Where was her hope of ever getting to lead the life *she* wanted?

"*Kumm* on in!" Ned Schmidt's booming voice

called out from the front porch of his house. "Time to *kumm* in and get the *sing* started!"

Sadie hurried to her feet and announced, "*Danki* for the water, Aaron. I guess I'll see you around." She made her way to the house quickly, stepping across the lush spring grass with her bare feet, her shoes held in her hands.

She didn't look back to see what Aaron was doing. She just wanted to get away from him as quickly as possible.

Still seated on the grass where he had joined Sadie, Aaron felt frozen in place. He wore a scrunched-up frown as he watched Sadie practically sprint toward the house. He couldn't understand her point of view at all. How could she think of ever leaving the Amish? Aaron had never dreamed of turning away from the community that he loved. He had always known that the Amish lifestyle was just what he wanted, with its simple, pure, and innocent ways. The outside world seemed so exhausting and rushed, while the Amish community was like a relaxing, calming glass of sweet tea.

Unfortunately, despite Aaron's certainty about his faith, he was also no stranger to those who left the faith. His elder sister, Bridget, had done just that when she was on her *Rumspringa*. It was a decision that had broken his parents' hearts and almost tore their family apart. And now it turned out that Sadie was bent on walking the same path? How was Aaron supposed to accept the fact that the girl he found the most attractive was so opposed to his lifestyle and his most precious faith?

Forcing himself to his feet, Aaron made his way into the house, where the other young folk were already gathered around the table, laughing together and enjoying snacks. Choosing a seat next to Joe, Aaron was able to catch a glimpse here and there of Sadie sitting at the other end of the long wooden table. She looked very lonely as she sat by herself, and for the first time, Aaron realized how sad she seemed. He'd always been so enamored by her beauty that he hadn't taken the time to perceive that she also seemed quite unhappy. Frowning, he wondered exactly what he could do to help her learn to love the Amish way of life and hopefully learn to love him in the process.

Aaron let his mind travel across all the possibilities as the night progressed, but it felt like he was coming up short. By the time he finally decided to stop worrying about it, the *sing* was coming to a close and night was beginning to wrap its arms around the small community.

When Aaron walked out to his buggy, he tried to catch sight of Sadie, but his gaze only landed on her in time to see her climbing up into her grandfather's buggy. Watching Sadie settle down next to Bishop Kauffman, Aaron wondered if she had ever let her family know how dissatisfied she was with the Amish way of life. Surely, it would break her father's heart to know that the only one he had left in the world was ready to desert him as well.

Making his way to his waiting buggy, Aaron climbed up on the seat and clicked his tongue for the horse to move forward. His elder brother, Amos, who was courting, was directing his buggy out on the road with his girlfriend at his side.

"Well, Ginger," Aaron spoke to his horse as she trotted along. "Looks like it's just you and me again tonight. Hope you're not getting sick of me."

The horse didn't respond, and Aaron chuckled. While he doubted Ginger minded one way or the other, he had to admit that he was getting tired of riding home by himself. What he wouldn't give to have Sadie at his side.

Unfortunately, that seemed unlikely to ever happen.

Chapter Five

Settling in the buggy next to her grandfather, Sadie leaned her back against the hardwood plank seatback and prepared herself for the long trip home. As if it wasn't bad enough to have to go to the *sings*, being escorted there and back by her grandfather made it that much worse.

"You know, *Groossdaadi*," Sadie started slowly as she reached down to finger her blue dress between her thumb and index finger, "I am the only *maedel* at the *sing* who has to be escorted there and back again by my *groossdaadi*."

"*Ya*," Grandfather Kauffman shot back with a knowing look as he glanced at her over his wireframe glasses, "but you're the only *maedel* there who is an only *kind*. Most of them have older *schweschdre* or *brieder* to ride with."

Emitting a deep sigh, Sadie muttered, "I'm

sure that I would be perfectly fine driving back and forth by myself. If you and *Daed* would trust me once in a while, perhaps I'd enjoy the young peoples' gatherings more."

It was true. Having to be shuttled back and forth like a little child was belittling and annoying. What Sadie wouldn't give to drive herself to the events and enjoy the silent evening rides alone.

Clearing his throat, the bishop shot back, "Perhaps if you would get your head out of the clouds and get a boyfriend, you would enjoy them even more. Then I wouldn't have to drive you back and forth."

The barbed comment had its desired effect on Sadie, yet she found her thoughts traveling back to Aaron Miller and his obvious attempts at befriending her. If Sadie wasn't so dead set against the possibility of having an attachment in the community, Aaron would certainly be a nice excuse to get away from her cantankerous grandfather.

Almost as if he needed to drive his point home, Bishop Kauffman went on to say, "Sadie, I hope you realize that you are eighteen years old. You're not getting any younger."

"*Ya, Groossdaadi.*" Sadie replied, unable to

restrain from rolling her eyes and hoping he wouldn't see it in the light of the moon. "I know how old I am."

"And at eighteen, you should be looking for a young *mann* with whom to settle down." Pointing a bony finger in her direction, he explained, "At your age, it's time to get baptized and plan your future in the *gmay*."

Each word that her grandfather spoke was another barb to her wounded psyche. She hated it when he started talking about her responsibilities to the Amish community; stuck beside him on the buggy, she was a reluctant captive audience.

"Your *maem* was so much like you." At this assertion, Sadie sat up a bit straighter and listened carefully. She so rarely heard anyone talk about her mother that she was anxious to hang on to every word.

"My *dochder*, Sarah, was headstrong just like you. *Ya*, you may not have ever had the chance to know her, but you act just like her. Maybe that's why I try so hard to protect you."

The words actually soothed some of her grandfather's previous barbs. He didn't seem quite as harsh when she thought of him trying to protect her. Then, almost as if he delighted in destroying a pleasant moment, Bishop Kauffman added, "My Sarah took a long time to get married. And I feel that is what killed her." Shaking his head slowly, he frowned and reached up to run a hand through his gray beard as he went on to say, "She was older than most of the other *maed* in the *gmay* when she got married and even older when she discovered she was pregnant. I am sure that it was because of her age that she had so much trouble with her pregnancy and then delivery. You know, she died giving birth to you, Sadie...because she waited too long."

All of Sadie's fuzzy feelings toward her grandfather evaporated instantly. She should have known that there would be some sort of underlying intention behind his seemingly heartfelt words.

"Losing my only *dochder* broke my heart," he went on to say. "I had already lost my *fraa,* and then to lose my *dochder*? Surely, you will do the same thing to your *daed* if you don't choose a different path. Surely, he will also mourn the loss of his *fraa* and *dochder* if you continue to wait to get married and have *kinner*."

Gritting her teeth, Sadie tried to hold her temper at bay. Her grandfather was so superstitious and ridiculous! How could he think that age played any role in her mother's death when she knew dozens of *Englisch* women who had babies when they were much older?

"Don't you want your *daed* to live long enough to see his *kinnskinner*?" Bishop Kauffman pressed, seemingly trying a different tactic. "Sadie, when *Gott* made Adam and Eve, He told them to be fruitful and multiply. You need to think about how you are going to fulfill the Lord's commands."

Not giving her time to respond, her grandfather rushed ahead to add, "At your age, to have no suitor, I have to think that you haven't come up with a plan. If you want to make the Lord happy, then you will find someone to marry, have *kinner*, and raise your *familye* in the *Amisch* faith."

As he continued to drone on, Sadie simply listened silently. She didn't think that she had it in her to be the woman that he required of her. She knew what she wanted out of life, and it certainly didn't involve the Amish faith—in fact, if she were honest, it might not involve God at all.

Closing her eyes, Sadie simply counted down the minutes until she would get home and forced herself to endure the long, annoying lecture that her grandfather seemed bent on providing. As he talked, she smiled in secret satisfaction at the realization that his comments were actually doing more to push her in the opposite direction. While he babbled on about the need for early marriages, Sadie considered how likely it would have been that her mother would have lived if she had given birth in a hospital.

Sadie hadn't been told much about her birth, but she knew that her mother had been under the care of a midwife. When it became obvious that she needed more medical help, someone had to run to a phone shanty to call the ambulance. By the time the paramedics arrived, it was too late to save her. She had already hemorrhaged and passed away.

Swallowing against the bitter lump in her throat, Sadie secretly cursed the lifestyle that had taken her mother from her too early.

Aaron waited a minute for his eyes to adjust to the dimmer light in his grandfather's workshop as he stepped inside. Abe Miller was in his mid-seventies and far past retirement, but he still enjoyed running a small workshop where he repaired buggies. The work kept him from getting bored and provided some extra money for him and his wife.

"*Gude daag, Groossdaadi*!" Aaron called out, glancing around the dusty workshop.

Abe stepped out of the back room, carrying a buggy wheel under one arm. He smiled at his grandson cheerfully and pushed his wireframe glasses up on his nose as he exclaimed, "*Ach*! What a *wunderbaar* surprise. I didn't expect to see you today, Aaron. What brings you out this way?"

Shrugging his shoulders, Aaron contemplated where to start. He leaned his shoulder against one of the poles in the barn and said, "Well, I finished on the construction job early today. We thought it was going to rain, so we took off early. Thought it'd be a *gut* opportunity to *kumm* by and talk to you."

His grandfather's mien said it all—Abe Miller didn't believe Aaron's excuse for one second. Smirking, Aaron added, "Plus, I felt like I needed a little advice...from someone I know is older and wiser."

Abe chuckled and quipped, "Well, I can't promise that I'm wiser, but I sure am older! What's on your mind?"

For as long as he could remember, Aaron had always gone to his grandfather for help with life's greatest difficulties. While his parents might scold him and try to tell him what to do, Grandpa Abe was always ready to simply offer some words of wisdom without pressuring him to do something he didn't want to, leaving him to choose his path.

Running his finger against the wooden beam, Aaron considered how to begin. "Well, there's this *maedel* that I'm trying to talk to." As soon as the words left Aaron's lips, a surge of bashfulness overwhelmed him. It didn't help that his grandfather's grin had tripled in size.

"Woman troubles are the worst," Abe replied sympathetically as he stepped forward to slap Aaron on the back. "But what seems to be the issue?"

Sighing, Aaron explained, "Well, it's Sadie Renno...Jacob's *dochder*."

Abe's face clouded over, and he shook his head slowly. "She's a beautiful *maedel*, but I've always thought she seemed so sad and lonely."

Nodding, Aaron's heart grew heavy as he admitted, "*Ya*, I think that describes her well. She is very forlorn. And when I tried to talk to her the other night, she made it sound like she's dissatisfied with her life amongst the *Amisch*. I'm afraid that she's likely to leave!"

Eyeing Aaron with concern, Abe asked, "You wouldn't let her lead you away from the faith, would you?"

Horrified at the mere idea of it, Aaron exclaimed, "*Ach*! *Nee*! I would never do that! I would not consider a relationship with someone who would turn her back on our lifestyle and faith." Thinking of his elder sister who had left the faith, Aaron added, "I'm not like Bridget. But I do... worry for Sadie." Recounting his earlier attempts to talk to his brother, he said, "I talked to Amos about it, and he thinks I should try to convince her that she's wrong. But I don't think that's the way to get her to pay attention to me."

Chortling at the mere thought of it, Abe shook his head and reached up to rub his nose as he said, "Amos has a lot to learn about women! *Nee*, if you want a *maedel* to listen to your opinion, then you need to listen to hers first. I think your best bet is to simply listen to her and let her explain to you what she finds so disturbing about the *Amisch* lifestyle. If you listen to what makes her upset and allow her to pour out her heart, then she will be more willing to listen to your suggestions." Reaching out to poke a finger against Aaron's chest, he warned, "Just you make sure that you don't get swayed by her!"

Smiling in agreement, Aaron crossed his heart with his index finger and said, "I promise I won't do that! *Danki* so much for the advice, *Groossdaadi*."

Pointing toward the wheel, Abe said, "I've got to get this wheel finished, but you can sit here and talk to me. Now that you've got your deepest secret off your chest, how about we talk about what else you've been up to?"

As he sat down on a wooden stool and watched his grandfather work, Aaron found an unfamiliar sense of hope settling over him where Sadie was concerned. Perhaps there really was a chance that he would be able to befriend Sadie and show her that the Amish lifestyle was truly the one in which she belonged.

If not, then Aaron was going to have to simply give her up. He was much too devoted to God to ever consider turning his back on all that mattered most to him.

Chapter Six

A cloud of dust rose out of the rug as Sadie stood on her porch and beat a stick against it, causing her to choke out a cough.

"If we were *Englisch*, we could have a vacuum cleaner," Sadie muttered bitterly to herself. She had been lucky enough to take on several cleaning jobs for *Englisch* families during her teenage years, and Sadie quickly embraced all the modern conveniences that their homes had to offer.

How much easier her work would be if she had a vacuum cleaner, a washing machine, and a dishwasher! Sadie was convinced she would enjoy her chores more if she could use some of those time-saving appliances and have time left to do things other than menial tasks.

Straightening, she prepared to hit the rug again. At least she could take some of her frustrations out on it!

"*Gude daag,* there!"

The voice startled Sadie, and she turned around in surprise. There, standing against the porch railing, was Aaron Miller. He held an apple in one hand and wore a pleasant smile on his face.

"*Ach*!" Sadie exclaimed, lowering her stick. "You nearly scared me to death!"

"Well, you nearly hit me with that big stick!" Aaron teased with a playful grin.

There was something about his easygoing manner that drew Sadie to him more than the previous night. He had seemed so ill-at-ease at the *sing,* while now he seemed more confident. Looking around, she sought out a horse and buggy. As if he could read her thoughts, Aaron supplied, "I walked. I thought it seemed like a *gut* day for it. After all, the sun's shining, and the sky is clear."

"*Ya,*" she agreed. "I guess it would be a *gut* day for that."

Shrugging, Aaron suggested, "*Kumm* with me. I'm just going down the lane to see if the wildflowers are blooming yet."

Surprisingly, the invitation actually sounded somewhat enticing. Sadie could certainly use a chance to get away from the house and her chores for a few minutes. But, on the other hand, she knew that she needed to be firm about her resolve to avoid Aaron.

Sadie was actually amazed that he wanted to see her after she had laid bare her heart at the *sing* the previous night. She had been convinced that he would keep his distance for good once he knew that she was dissatisfied with the Amish lifestyle.

As if fate was going to help make up her mind, the front door swung open, and Jacob Renno stuck his head out to announce, "I forgot to tell you, Sadie. Your *groossdaadi* is coming over any time now to pick up that old hay rake in the barn. He said that if you were home, he wanted to talk to both of us...something about finishing a conversation you had last night..."

Instant dread filled Sadie's heart at the thought of having to continue talking about her supposed urgency to get married young and start having babies immediately. Suddenly, she was anxious for any excuse to get away from the house. She looked back toward Aaron and then at her father before announcing, "*Ach*, I was about to take a walk with Aaron Miller, here. He came all the way to ask me. Would you mind if I skipped out on this visit?"

Jacob's gaze traveled to Aaron, and Sadie espied a spark of hope fill his eyes. Giving an enthusiastic nod, he smiled and said, "That would be fine! I had no idea you had plans."

Sadie grimaced inwardly at the excitement in her father's eyes; she knew what he was thinking, but on the other hand, she also knew that she had to do something to get away. Hurrying off the porch, she joined Aaron as they made their way down the gravel driveway and back toward the road. They reached the blacktop just as she heard Bishop Kauffman's buggy rattling up the road. Releasing a sigh of relief, Sadie was so glad that she had managed to avoid another of his long lectures. She didn't think she would be able to stand it if he got her father involved in the criticism as well.

"*Ach*, it might have been fate that you got here when you did!" Sadie said with a laugh as she walked alongside Aaron.

"Not the biggest fan of your *groossdaadi*?"

Shaking her head, Sadie let out a chuckle and said, "I think it's more that he's not a big fan of me." The wind picked up and grabbed her prayer *kapp*, and she had to put her hand on her head to hold it down. "My *groossdaadi* is a *gut* bishop, but he's a strict *mann* to have in the *familye*. He always manages to make me feel like I don't quite meet his expectations."

Rather than criticize her, Aaron simply kept his peace. Sadie found herself appreciating someone who could listen to her gripe without trying to convince her to feel some other way.

"Have you always had trouble with your *familye*?" Aaron asked.

Feeling a little like she had made them seem worse than they were, Sadie hurried to say, "I wouldn't say they're really trouble. They just try to overprotect me." Sobering even more, she added, "I've often felt like if my *maem* were still alive, things would have been very different. They say that she was a lot like me. She wasn't interested in getting married and had a pull toward the fancy things in life. But in the end, she gave in and married my *daed*...and we all see where that got her. Six feet under in the cemetery." Sadie realized that hot tears had pooled in her eyes. She wished that she could somehow stop them before they overwhelmed her.

"Look." Aaron pointed toward a bank alongside the road. "The flowers are out."

Sure enough, the grassy spot was dotted with a beautiful carpet of pink, purple, red, and yellow.

"Looks like a rainbow," Sadie sighed in awe, momentarily distracted from the depressing thoughts that were plaguing her mind.

Nodding, Aaron gave her a knowing look as he said, "And *Gott* made every color of the rainbow with a reason—even if some of them might look like they might not go well together. It's all part of the Lord's creation. Just like you are."

The words were unexpected, and they managed to touch a part of Sadie's soul deep within. It was the first time that someone seemed to appreciate her for who she was rather than simply trying to change her and fit her into a generic mold.

Giving Aaron a genuine smile, Sadie discovered that she was actually pleased he had invited her on the walk, and it wasn't just because she wanted an escape from her grandfather. For a moment, she wondered if perhaps she and Aaron might actually become friends. As quickly as the thought flittered through her mind, she brushed it aside—she didn't have any room for forming attachments if she was going to leave the Amish faith. And that was exactly what she planned to do.

∞∞∞

Sauntering back to the Renno house with Sadie at his side, Aaron hardly noticed how tired and achy his legs had become. He had followed his grandfather's advice, and it truly seemed to have made a difference. By listening to Sadie and paying attention to her complaints rather than trying to immediately fight them, it seemed that he had been able to open a door to her soul.

Considering his sister Bridget once more, his heart ached within his chest. Bridget might have been four years Aaron's senior, but she had been an important part of his life. He had been so stunned when she left the Amish to join the wild world of the *Englischers* that he was never quite the same.

Bridget hadn't been the only one to leave their Amish community, but she had been the one who affected his family the most. Aaron could only hope that Sadie wouldn't be next in line to crush his heart and run away to join the unknown. Perhaps if he could become her friend, he would at least have the opportunity to make an impression on her and show her that their faith life could be more than the rules and regulations she heard from her grandfather.

But in the meantime, Aaron also knew that he was going to have to be careful not to put his heart on the line. With Sadie's bent toward the *Englisch*, he couldn't let himself get too attached.

"I'm glad to see that *Groossdaadi* is gone," Sadie commented as they neared her house and saw the empty yard.

Nodding, Aaron said, "I'm glad you agreed to go on a walk with me."

"Me too," Sadie concurred. "It was actually fun."

Smiling at her, Aaron asked, "Would you be up for a buggy ride tomorrow night?"

It was apparent that Sadie was completely taken aback by his question, by her squirming. She let out a laugh and said, "I don't know about that... I'd have to think about it." While it certainly wasn't the reply that Aaron wanted, at least it wasn't an outright rejection.

Grasping for every bit of hope that he could find, Aaron said, "How about I stop by and see how you feel after I get off work?"

Looking up at him, Sadie gave him the slightest hint of a smile and nodded. "*Ach*. I guess it wouldn't hurt to give it a try. I'm supposed to be shopping for a while tomorrow, but I should be home in plenty of time."

Unable to stop his smile from spreading, Aaron replied, "Then I guess we'll just wait and see what happens tomorrow."

Chapter Seven

Sadie's gaze wandered over the items displayed on the shelves as she made her way through the aisles of the small Amish store. Every Tuesday, her father let her walk down to Girod's General Store, where she picked up things they needed around the house.

Glancing at the sparse display of available sugar, she wished that she could simply jump into a car and drive herself to town to pick up a bag of the powdered sugar needed for the cake she was planning on baking.

"Someday..." she whispered under her breath, her mind wandering to the day when she would be free to do whatever she wanted without the confines of the Amish community holding her back.

The front door of the store swung open, and Sadie looked up to see who might be coming in.

Rather than being the usual Amish customers, this new arrival was a young man with a confident strut. His short brown hair was combed back and styled to perfection, while a pair of sunglasses covered his eyes.

There was something about him that took Sadie's breath away—as if he commanded an air of dignity that couldn't be ignored.

Pushing his sunglasses back on his head, he let out a low whistle and muttered, "Wow. A place frozen in time."

He glanced in Sadie's direction and gave a nod in the way of a greeting before picking up his pace and marching through the store.

Sadie tried to look back at her purchase but felt her eyes surreptitiously travel to the stranger. He seemed to be quite at home in the store, taking long strides toward the back of the building, where he pushed aside a curtain and stepped directly into the back room.

Grabbing a bag of sugar, Sadie heard the voice of Bertha Girod cry out, "Jensen! You're back!"

Jensen Girod. While he had been several years older than Sadie, she could still remember when he left their Amish faith to join the *Englisch*. It had been a huge scandal, with him leaving right before

Bridget Miller decided to leave as well.

Her curiosity piqued, Sadie wondered what had happened to bring him back to the community. Could he have decided to come back so that he could rejoin the faith? Surely, no one would be ignorant enough to do that! She figured that once someone had the chance to taste the pleasures of the modern world, they wouldn't return back to their plain roots.

Sadie tried to secretly listen to the conversation taking place in the back room, but her eavesdropping was cut short when Josiah Girod came bursting from the back room with a perplexed look on his face. Not even giving Sadie time to collect herself, he announced, "I'm sorry, but the store is going to have to close early today."

Sadie opened her mouth to speak, but it was too late. The owner of the store was practically pushing her out the door, not giving her a chance to even pay for her groceries or take them with her.

As Sadie stepped out onto the country store's porch, she heard the door slam shut behind her. The sound of it locking made her raise her eyebrows, and she felt a little annoyed.

"Well," she said as she put her hands on her hips, "looks like I won't be getting my baking done after all." The two mile walk back home might be easier without groceries to carry, but it certainly made the journey seem more futile.

As she walked, Sadie's mind wandered back toward Jensen Girod and his surprise return to the community. With her grandfather being the bishop, she could only hope that she would have a chance to find out what had brought him back to the Amish and just how long he intended to stay.

The sound of a car approaching behind her prompted Sadie to slow down and move over to the side of the road so that it could pass. To her surprise, the driver didn't continue; instead, he simply slowed down more.

Feeling slightly concerned, Sadie turned to look at the driver of the shiny black sports car. The tinted window rolled down to reveal Jensen Girod peering out at her. He was wearing his sunglasses again but hurried to push them up on his forehead.

"*Gude daag,* there," he said with a charming smile. "I'm sorry I disrupted your shopping experience today. I didn't expect my parents to take things so far." Frowning, he added, "You didn't even get any of your shopping done, did you?"

Shrugging a shoulder, Sadie felt out of place

and uncomfortable as she admitted, "*Nee*, but that's fine. All I really needed was a bag of powdered sugar."

His car now pulled to a stop, Jensen clicked a button to unlock the doors and said, "Hop in. I'll run you to the grocery store in town, and then I'll take you back home."

"*Ach*, I couldn't put you out like that—" Sadie started to say with a shake of her head.

Unwilling to take no for an answer, the young man held up a hand and said, "You've got to. It's the only thing that will make me feel better after what happened. I feel so bad about that. I had no clue my parents would react like that."

Smiling softly, Sadie grabbed for the door handle and said, "Well, I guess I should take you up on your offer, then."

Jensen smiled a smile that could have melted the hardest of hearts as Sadie opened the door and climbed in. Sitting down on the cool leather, she took in the comfort of the fancy automobile. While she was used to riding with paid *Englisch* drivers on occasion, she certainly wasn't used to riding in style like this!

Glancing over at Jensen, she had to secretly admit that the sugar was the last thing on her mind in that moment. She found Jensen fascinating and was just glad for a chance to get to know someone who had escaped their strict community.

"I don't think I know you," Jensen announced as he stuck out a hand. "I'm Jensen Guthrie... it used to be Girod before I left the *Amisch*." Chuckling to himself, he added, "Girod isn't really a name you hear much in the modern world, so I learned to ditch that one quick!"

Taking his hand in her own, Sadie shook it gently as she replied, "I'm Sadie Renno." Something about Jensen made her uncomfortable yet also intrigued. Since he was at least six years older than she was, she remembered little about him when he was in the Amish community. All she could remember was an older boy who never seemed to fit in with the other young folk and who had a propensity for trouble.

Looking at Jensen now, it was hard not to stare. He certainly didn't look like the Amish boy that she could remember from the past with a bowl haircut and suspenders. Instead, he seemed like he belonged right in the modern world.

"My *groossdaadi* is Bishop Abron Kauffman." Sadie made the announcement before she could think better of it. She was so used to announcing him to those who didn't know her. Everyone knew her grandfather! As soon as the words slipped off her tongue, she wished that she could take them back. She seriously doubted that Jensen would have very good memories of her grandfather.

Sure enough, Jensen's expression instantly soured. Pausing for a moment, he finally said, "Well, I feel sorry for you if that's the case."

Leaning back against her seat, Sadie realized that she felt sorry for herself too. Her grandfather was a hard man—everyone knew it. And he certainly was hard on her as well.

"It's not easy," she finally muttered under her breath as she looked out the window to watch trees whizzing by. Shaking her head, she added, "You're the lucky one in this situation."

Jensen laughed and raised an eyebrow as he asked, "Do I detect some jealousy in your voice?"

Meeting his gaze with a sigh, Sadie determined that she might as well be honest with Jensen. After all, while he might be a stranger, he had surely still walked a similar road during his years of *Rumspringa*.

"I won't be *Amisch* forever," Sadie declared, watching Jensen carefully to see how he took the news. "I have every intention of leaving this life as soon as I possibly can. I don't intend to spend the rest of my life as a barefooted, pregnant *fraa* with a *mann* telling me what to do."

Eyeballing her sideways, Jensen bluntly asked, "What's holding you back?"

What was holding Sadie back? The list was too long to even start naming things. She shrugged her shoulders and explained, "I guess it just seems like everything is stacked against me."

Jensen nodded and frowned as if he could empathize with her plight. "Yeah, that's true. I think the church leaders plan it that way...they try to make it so difficult to leave this stupid cult that it's hard to do even when you want to. I looked at the big modern world, and it seemed overwhelming at first, but once I actually took the plunge, it wasn't so difficult. It became more of an exciting challenge."

"But what did you do about getting a birth certificate or a Social Security card?" Sadie felt like a massive door of opportunity that had previously been triple bolted had finally been opened now that there was a source of information to help her with all her questions about joining the modern world. She wanted to cling to Jensen and glean all the answers that she possibly could from him.

Cocking his head to one side and looking ahead almost unseeing, he appeared transported back in time. Finally, he said, “Well, I hit the jackpot with that one since I was born in a hospital. I just had to get copies of my birth certificate and Social Security card. There were hoops to jump through but nothing too bad. It was well worth the struggle. As soon as I got those, I was able to get a driver’s license and a job that was better than just odd work—then I got my own place and started college. I’m now working as an architect, and as you can see”—he held his hand out to motion toward the car in which they were sitting—“all my struggles certainly paid off. I now have the world at my fingertips.”

Jensen’s declaration was simultaneously comforting and overwhelming. Would she actually be able to take on the challenges ahead of her and grasp the big world?

Reaching up to rub the bridge of her nose, she scoffed, “It might be more than I can ever do.”

In a movement that shocked her, Jensen reached out and put his hand on top of hers. Giving her hand a squeeze that made her look up to meet his eyes, Jensen’s face was full of mingled sympathy and understanding.

"When you decide you want to leave, I'll be here for you." He said it so sincerely and full of honest compassion that Sadie's bitter attitude dissipated to one of hope and anticipation.

Letting go of her hand, Jensen navigated the steering wheel while he fished in his pocket. Pulling out a business card, he handed it to her and said, "My number's on the front of it."

Perusing the card, Sadie read off his name and some information about his work. Giving a grateful nod, she smiled and said, "*Danki*. I might do just that."

Pulling up next to the store, Jensen returned her smile and said, "Now run in there and get your stuff. I'll be waiting out here."

Hurrying out of the car, Sadie rushed into the store and grabbed the few things that she needed. Making her way back out, she felt almost surprised to see Jensen's car still parked alongside the curb, waiting on her. Somehow, she had expected him to have disappeared, nothing more than a dream or a figment of her imagination. It seemed almost too good to be true that someone as handsome and as knowledgeable as him would be paying attention to her.

Climbing into the car, she held up her bag and said, "Success."

Putting down the phone that he had been looking at, he put his hands back on the steering wheel and smiled at her. "Well, I have got to get to a job, so I'll go on and get you home."

Riding along down the familiar country roads, Sadie found herself wishing that she could have more time with the ex-Amish young man. She wanted to learn all that he could tell her about the *Englisch* world, but more than anything, she just wanted to spend time with him. She felt a connection with him that she felt with no other.

"Don't get too close to my house," Sadie warned him as he turned onto her road. "Just park here, and I'll walk the rest of the way." As she gathered her groceries, an overwhelming urge to ask him to simply take her with him surged through her. She hated to let him out of her sight.

As if he was feeling the same thing, Jensen asked, "Do you think there's any chance I'll get to see you again before I leave?"

Biting down on her lower lip, Sadie shrugged and said, "*Ach*, I don't know. When are you leaving?"

"In two days," Jensen returned as he reached

up to run his well-manicured thumb against his steering wheel. "I'm here working on a project in a nearby town. I just thought I'd stop by to see my parents but…well, you can imagine how that went." He got a faraway look in his eyes as he explained, "All they seemed intent on doing was trying to convince me to come back to the *Amisch*." He let out a bitter laugh as he shook his head and declared, "Definitely not doing that!" Sitting up straighter, he turned his attention toward Sadie and suggested, "How about after I get done working tomorrow night, I'll meet up with you, and we can spend some time together?"

Glancing toward her father's house in the distance, Sadie couldn't help but wonder what he would say if he knew what she was thinking of doing. On the other hand, she couldn't let him rule her life forever. If she was truly going to break away from the Amish community, she was going to have to learn to start stepping out on her own now.

Nodding, she smiled and said, "*Ya*. I'll make it work…somehow."

Grinning from ear to ear, Jensen suggested, "I'll pick you up at this spot around seven tomorrow night. We can go get some pizza and talk more."

The idea sounded so daring yet at the same time so delightful. Sadie touched one hand to her chest to keep her heart from beating out of her chest as she reached for the door handle with the other and stepped out onto the pavement. Nodding, she said, "Well, I guess I'll see you then. Thanks for the ride."

Watching him drive away, Sadie felt frozen in place. Even with the promise of an upcoming dinner date, she didn't want to let him out of her sight. She wanted to cling to him—her only lifeline to a different world.

Closing her eyes, Sadie breathed in the fresh scents of the spring afternoon. Perhaps Jensen *was* her ticket to a different life—the type of life that she had always wanted. While she had a hard time believing in God, Jensen's arrival in town seemed almost providential.

When Jensen's car was out of sight, Sadie started the journey back toward her home. The afternoon was starting to turn into evening, and she needed to get the supplies into the house and check on supper.

As the house came into view, Sadie's walking on clouds ended instantaneously with a thud as she came back down to earth: there, parked right in front of her house, was the buggy of Aaron Miller. Frowning, she groaned. She had forgotten all about her promise to take a ride with Aaron.

Suddenly, all the softness that her heart had felt toward him was gone, and Sadie felt nothing but dread fill her entire body. In an instant, Aaron had become nothing more than a nuisance.

Chapter Eight

Aaron looked toward the house and shifted his weight in his seat as he sat impatiently in his buggy. He had just pulled up, but it appeared that Sadie was nowhere in sight. The front door opened, but rather than Sadie appearing, it was her father who stepped out onto the porch.

"*Gude daag,* Aaron!" Jacob called out as he raised a hand in greeting. "How are you today?"

Waving in return, Aaron tried to sound more enthusiastic than he felt as he explained, "*Ach,* doing well. Just got done with work. Sadie and I were supposed to go on a buggy ride this afternoon."

A strange expression crossed Jacob's face—one that seemed to be a mixture of hope and confusion.

"Well, she should be home any minute now,"

Jacob returned with a nod. “She just walked up to the Girods’ store. I don’t think she had much to get.”

Aaron tried not to let his uncertainty show as he sat there, turning his attention toward the road. He had taken his buggy right past the Girods’ store and didn’t see Sadie on the road. A deep sense of disquiet invaded the deepest part of his heart, and he wondered where Sadie could have gone. Was there a chance that she might have run away?

Just as his thoughts were starting to entertain the worst, Aaron saw Sadie’s form starting up the driveway, a few bags of groceries held at her side.

“*Gude daag,* Sadie!” Aaron called out as she approached his buggy. “I didn’t know if you’d remembered our ride or not.”

Sadie didn’t even attempt to smile. Instead, she just shrugged her shoulders and said, “*Ya,* I remembered. Things just took a little longer at the store than I expected.” Holding up her bags, she added, “I’ll just run these inside, and I’ll be right back.”

Watching her walk into the house, Aaron couldn’t help but notice how apathetic she seemed to be about taking a ride with him. While that wouldn’t have surprised him in the past, he truly had hoped that they made some progress towards a better relationship during their walk the previous day.

Squinting his eyes, Aaron noticed that the bags she was taking into the house bore the emblem from the grocery store in town rather than the Amish store up the road. She would have had to either take a buggy or hired a driver to take her that far in such a short amount of time. He knew it didn't matter where she got her groceries, yet at the same time, it compounded his discomfort and uncertainty. It felt like she was hiding something, and that clouded his heart over entirely.

You can't get too attached to her, Aaron told himself as she came back out of the house and started toward his buggy. *You're just going to have to be friends—you can't let her actually get to your heart.*

Aaron knew full well how Bridget had almost torn his parents' hearts right out of their chests. He couldn't let Sadie do the same to him. He was going to have to stay firm and distant no matter what.

∞∞∞

Riding alongside Aaron on the hard wooden seat of his buggy, Sadie found herself wishing that she had simply made up an excuse not to go with him. Perhaps she could have feigned fatigue to get her out of the trip. She was feeling rather emotionally drained with all that had transpired that afternoon.

Glancing at him out of the corner of her eye, Sadie couldn't help but notice how serious and aloof he seemed. Perhaps neither of them was truly in the mood for a leisurely buggy ride.

Allowing her gaze to travel to the wildflowers swaying in the breeze, Sadie considered trying to make small talk but then stopped herself. If Aaron wanted to ride with her, then he was going to have to be the one to start the conversation.

"Where were you off to today?" Aaron asked as if he had been able to hear her thoughts. But rather than being the same friendly attitude from the previous day, this time his question seemed abrupt and out of character. His tone sounded strangely suspicious and caused Sadie to bristle. Rather than seeming like a friendly ride, it was now feeling like she was being interrogated.

Shifting her weight in her seat, Sadie tried to hide her annoyance as she replied, "I went to the grocery store. I figured my *daed* would have told you that."

"*Ya*," Aaron agreed as he reached up to scratch at his forehead absent-mindedly. "He did tell me that. I guess I was just surprised to see that you were carrying grocery bags from the store in town. Isn't that a little far for you to walk?"

Sadie's annoyance multiplied as she considered the prying question. How dare Aaron Miller, who was no more than an acquaintance, suddenly start to act like she was his property?

Determined not to tell him anything other than what was necessary, she shrugged and illusively replied, "I suppose it might be."

Clicking his tongue to urge the horse forward, Aaron seemed to be contemplating her response. Dropping her chin into her hand, Sadie looked out across the rolling farmland. It looked so bright and inviting, even in the growing darkness of the evening. A butterfly flittered past the buggy, and she wished that she could be as carefree.

Glancing back towards Aaron, she wondered

what he would do if she came clean and admitted everything about her ride with Jensen. After all, Aaron was the one with whom she had shared her plans to leave the Amish from the start—he should be prepared for her to be making connections with ex-Amish and learning about how to leave the faith community. But on the other hand, Sadie feared that if she told him, he might share the news with her father—which would certainly put a stop to her upcoming visit with Jensen.

Aaron cleared his throat and said conversationally, "We had a new little filly born on the farm last night."

Sadie sat up straighter in her seat and could hardly help herself from saying, "*Ach*! That's always fun. I wish that *Daed* would let us raise some horses, but he's only interested in dairy cows and only wants a horse to pull the buggy."

Once Sadie broke free from the Amish, she would have some horses of her own, she silently promised herself. An image from the library magazine drifted through her mind, and Sadie considered what she would look like in a pair of blue jeans with her hair pulled back in a ponytail.

Aaron began to relay the details of the story, about arriving home just when the horse went into labor. They had been forced to call the vet to come help with the delivery since the filly was breech.

Sadie held her breath as she listened, enthralled; it felt like she was watching it all unfold right in front of her.

"I wish I could have been there," Sadie murmured before she could think better of her words. "I'd love to see a horse *kumm* into the world."

Aaron nodded and said, "*Ya*. It's truly a miracle." Cocking his head to one side, he added, "When you see something like that, it just helps you to remember that *Gott* really is real. You know miracles like that don't just happen by coincidence."

A strange surge of discomfort washed over Sadie at his words, and for some unknown reason, tears began to prick at her eyes. How easy Aaron made it sound! Faith seemed to come to him with no problem. A part of her wished that she could feel the same way instead of doubting the Lord at every turn. It was just hard to imagine how God could exist when her life had been so full of misfortune and sadness from the very start.

"If you'd like to *kumm* see the horses one day, I'd be happy to take you out to my parents' place to visit them," Aaron offered, pulling Sadie's mind away from her sad thoughts.

Shifting in her seat, she wondered how sensible it actually was for her to get closer to Aaron. After all, spending time around him was just setting them both up for heartache in the end. Now that she and Jensen had become acquainted, it seemed that everything in her life was about to change. Her dreams of leaving the Amish were becoming a reality.

"You could *kumm* see the new filly," Aaron said in a sing-song voice, almost as if he was trying to lure her.

Smiling the tiniest bit, Sadie reached up to push her bonnet back on her head, and she gave a small nod. "That might be fun."

Aaron grinned back at her as he asked, "How about tomorrow afternoon I *kumm* by your house and pick you up to *kumm* see it? My *maem* is supposed to be making a special dessert for supper, and *Daed* has said he might get out the ice cream maker. I'm sure they'd love to have you."

Tomorrow afternoon? Sadie already had plans with Jensen the following evening! She certainly couldn't stand her new friend up just to spend time with Aaron and his horses. Shaking her head, she hurried to turn down his invitation by saying, "I'm sorry, but tomorrow won't work. I already have something I need to do."

Aaron's brow furrowed, and he seemed discouraged, but then he forced himself to nod and said, "I guess we'll just have to do it some other day."

Kneading her hands together, Sadie hoped that she could make it through the rest of the ride without agreeing to any more meetings. While she enjoyed time with Aaron, she was realizing that their new friendship was simply growing into too much. If she was going to be leaving the Amish soon, there was no reason to try to foster a relationship that was only going to hurt them both.

Watching Sadie climb down from the wagon, Aaron felt his heart sink. He had come to her father's house with great expectations and hopes for their time together. After doing so much to break through her tough exterior the previous night, he had truly thought that things would be even better this time.

Unfortunately, it seemed destined to not be so.

The ride had started out badly with Aaron feeling like she was hiding something about her trip to the store, and his suspicions only grew during their ride. He had worked hard to give her the benefit of the doubt and push his misgivings aside, but it felt like his best attempts with her had fallen short.

Perhaps it was best that he simply had nothing else to do with Sadie Renno.

Even as the idea crossed his mind, a deep sense of loss pervaded Aaron's being. He hated the thought of giving up on Sadie—even if they had never truly started a relationship together.

"*Danki* for the ride," Sadie said courteously as her feet hit the ground.

Nodding, Aaron cleared his throat. A part of him was tempted to give up on Sadie, but another part of him clung desperately to the tiny seed of friendship that had sprouted. "Just because you can't *kumm* see the horses with me tomorrow doesn't mean you have to turn me down forever," Aaron announced, deciding to at least give things another try.

Sadie seemed to take in a deep breath. She

grabbed a hold of the buggy's side and looked up at him, her blue eyes squinting as she announced, "Aaron, I don't really mean to be rude or harsh, but I think I explained this the other day. I don't intend to be staying in the *gmay* much longer. Is there really any point in us spending time together?"

Swallowing hard, Aaron felt his fingers clasp tighter around the buggy reins as he suggested, "Maybe there's more reason than you realize—maybe we can at least be friends while you're here?"

Shrugging, Sadie seemed to contemplate his words before sighing deeply and saying, "I really just don't know that there's any point." She looked away into the distance as she admitted, "Don't tell my *daed*, please, but I've already got someone who's offered to help me leave if I want to."

Aaron's heart hit the ground with a thud. While he had known all along that Sadie was interested in leaving the Amish, knowing that she had someone offering to make the transition easier made it seem all the more likely that she would go through with her plans.

Giving him a sad smile, Sadie turned and walked toward the house, leaving him speechless and alone to battle his own hurt feelings and grapple with a dozen questions.

Chapter Nine

Sadie shifted from one foot to the other and pulled her shawl a little tighter against her body as she stood by the road at the same spot where Jensen had previously dropped her off. Although it had been a warm spring day, she could see her breath when she blew out into the night air. Glancing back toward her father's house, she spied a single light burning in the downstairs window.

"Hopefully, he won't notice I'm gone," she muttered to herself as she looked back toward the road.

She had claimed that she was tired right after the supper dishes were put away, giving her the perfect excuse to escape to her room for the night. Even now, standing alongside the road, Sadie wasn't sure whether to laugh or frown when she considered how she had climbed out of her window. In all her years, she had never done anything so daring.

Perhaps it's time for a lot of new experiences, Sadie thought to herself. She could only hope that Jensen would truly make good on his promise to come pick her up and wouldn't leave her standing along the side of the road while he forgot about her.

While Sadie wanted to believe that Jensen was above that, something deep inside of her made her doubt him and wonder if he truly deserved to be trusted entirely.

A dark sports car came into view, and Sadie's pulse accelerated. Stepping back off the paved road, she stood in the young grass and smiled when the car pulled to a stop beside her. The passenger window rolled down, and in the light of the car's interior, she found herself looking into the familiar eyes of Jensen.

"I was afraid you might change your mind," Jensen announced as he pushed a button to unlock the doors.

Shaking her head, Sadie smiled and assured him, "I'm not one to change my mind."

Pulling the door open, she allowed herself to slide into the leather seat. The car felt inviting after standing out in the cold, and she soaked in its warmth.

"Are you up for some pizza?" Jensen asked as he executed a U-turn and started back toward town.

Secretly wondering how she could possibly fit more food in her stomach after the meal of fried chicken that she had served her father, Sadie nodded her head and said, "*Ya*. But, more than that, I think I'm just anxious to talk."

Jensen glanced toward her as he maneuvered his car down the tiny country road and replied, "I'll just be glad to spend time with you, no matter what we're doing."

His words caught Sadie by surprise, and a blush darkened her cheeks. No one had ever openly complimented her like that before. It was a good feeling and one that she was sure she would cherish for the rest of her life. Watching Jensen out of the corner of her eye, she wondered if there was any chance that he might be a part of her life more long term than simply this one night. If he was offering to help her leave the Amish, might he be a part of her life for years to come? The mere thought made her heart leap, and for the first time, it seemed possible that Sadie's future might truly involve both love and the modern lifestyle she had always wanted.

∞∞∞

Even though the pizzeria was empty, Sadie still felt nervous when she stepped in through the front door. While Jensen seemed more than confident of himself while he asked for a seat in a corner booth, Sadie didn't miss the way that the server openly eyeballed her. Surely, it looked strange for an *Englischer* and an Amish girl to be eating together.

Once they were alone with a large thick-crusted pizza between them, Jensen finally asked, "Are you really serious about leaving the *Amisch*?"

Taking a delicate bite of her pizza, Sadie nodded and said, "I am. I guess it's been in my mind since I was a little *maedel*. When I was around ten years old, I had a chance to look at a magazine, and it just changed my entire view of the world around us." Narrowing her eyes, she could remember exactly how she felt sitting in the library, peeking through the forbidden magazine. "I realized that the *Englisch* world can be amazing and inviting—not some evil place to fear."

Jensen was nodding in agreement as he grabbed another slice of pizza and put it on his plate. "I can totally understand. The church leaders try so hard to make it seem like everything modern is terrible...when it's not that way at all. Everything is simply a tool to better help humanity."

"Why did you decide to leave the *Amisch*?" Sadie asked, her own curiosity coming to the fore.

Chuckling, Jensen took a bite of his pizza and chewed it, obviously mulling over his words before finally admitting, "It was a lot of things, really. Actually, I don't think I had ever considered leaving until I was a teenager. I had always thought I would just stay *Amisch* forever. Then, when I turned sixteen, I got a job working on a horse farm that belonged to some *Englischers*. I had so much fun—not so much with the horses but with the other guys. We started hanging out more and more, and it started to feel like everything I considered fun was suddenly against the rules of the *Amisch*." Shrugging his shoulders, he finally finished by saying, "In the end, I got fed up with having my parents and the church leaders try to control me. I didn't like getting nagged about everything I enjoyed doing. I started looking at the possibility of leaving and realized that the *Englisch* world actually had more to offer me than staying *Amisch*."

Considering his words, Sadie realized that they were looking at things from totally different perspectives. Unable to hold back the one question that plagued her the most, she asked, "Do you ever have any regrets about leaving?"

Jensen let out an outright laugh, and he shook his head as he reached for his Coke. "Absolutely not!" Crossing his arms on the table, he met Sadie's gaze and said, "I now have a college education and a super successful job. I make a lot of money, and I have the things I want, when I want them. The world is at my fingertips. What would I have done if I had stayed *Amisch*?"

Studying Jensen, Sadie tried to picture him working in his parents' grocery store. Surely, he would be stuck living a regular Amish existence, helping on the farm and stocking shelves, still dressed in his plain Amish clothes and driving a horse and buggy. It would be such a far cry from the exciting life he now led.

Cocking his head to one side, Jensen seemed to be assessing things before admitting, "But sometimes...like right now, I realize that there are some things I might be missing out on." Allowing his fingers to slowly slide across the table until they touched hers, he said, "There have never been any prettier girls in the *Englisch* world. You, Sadie Renno, take the prize."

If Sadie had thought she was blushing earlier, it felt like her face was truly on fire right then. She had to look down at the table to keep from melting into a puddle of mingled delight and embarrassment.

"You've done something to me, Sadie," Jensen assured her as he let his fingers wrap over hers and gave her hand a tender squeeze. "I have to leave to go back to New York City in the morning, but I don't want this to be the last time that I get to see you. Are you really serious about leaving?"

Suddenly, Sadie felt herself feeling unsure about everything. Was Jensen going to ask her to leave with him the next day? What would she do if he did ask such a thing?

"I'm coming back in a few weeks to finish up my architecture project," Jensen explained as he ran his thumb back and forth against her fingers. "Will you leave with me when I come back?"

Tears pooled in Sadie's eyes as she thought about the choice that lay in front of her. It felt like she had been offered the golden goose of opportunity, yet she was too scared to take it. Slowly nodding, she had to use her free hand to reach up to wipe her eyes as she whispered, "*Ya. Ya*, I will come with you. That would truly be the greatest opportunity of my life."

And in that moment, Sadie knew that while she might not be leaving her hometown immediately, she had finally taken the first step toward embracing the life that she had always wanted. Thanks to Jensen, she would get the opportunity to finally be a part of the *Englisch* world and fulfill the dream that had taken root in her heart when she was a little girl thumbing through a magazine.

Chapter Ten

Sadie was relieved to see the house in complete darkness when she reached the doorstep of her home. She didn't need a watch to know that time had quickly gotten away from her when she was out with Jensen. After they had finished their pizza, they drove the backroads together, simply talking and enjoying each other's company.

Goodbye had been painful, and even now, Sadie felt tears moistening her eyes when she remembered how it had hurt to see him driving away. While Jensen had promised that he would return and take her with him, she couldn't help but wonder if he truly would. Once he got to New York City, it seemed it would be so easy to get caught up in the hustle and bustle of life and his work—she wondered if he would even remember her at all.

Pushing the front door of the house open slowly, Sadie tiptoed inside and shut it behind her as quietly as possible. Breathing another sigh of relief, she wished that she believed in God more firmly so that she could thank Him for keeping her father from discovering that she was gone!

Making her way slowly to the steps, she lifted one foot and prepared to lift her weight up to the second when a voice made her freeze in place.

"Sadie. Where have you been?"

Sadie would have known her father's voice anywhere, and hearing it made her instantly feel sick to her stomach. Turning slowly, she saw him sitting at the kitchen table. With a flick of his hand, he lit a match and proceeded to illuminate the room by taking it to a lantern wick.

"*Kumm*, Sadie," he announced, motioning toward the table. "Looks like we need to talk."

Sadie's mind was going as fast as Jensen's speedy sports car as she turned and slowly made her way toward the table. Like a trapped rabbit, she was trying to think of any way to escape the situation at hand.

The lantern illuminated the entire room, revealing the exhausted face of her father. Jacob Renno looked tired from worry and lack of sleep, but more than that, he looked angry and stern.

"Where have you been, Sadie?" Jacob asked, his tone firm.

Shrugging her shoulders, she tried to appear nonchalant as she said, "I just went with someone to get some pizza. I wasn't doing anything wrong." Lifting her hands as if to prove her innocence, she explained, "After all, *Daed*, I'm not a little *maedel*. I'm an eighteen-year-old *maedel* on her *Rumspringa*. I deserve to do a few things."

"If it was innocent, then why did it have to be a secret?" Jacob pressed, staring at her like a judge about to convict a criminal. "Why did you have to sneak out through your window without telling me?"

Trying her best to build her case, Sadie exclaimed, "*Ach, Daed*, I have to! For goodness' sake, I'm not allowed to do anything unless I sneak out to do it. I can't even ride to *sings* by myself—*Groossdaadi* has to take me! I have to even beg to walk to the store alone." She hoped that her story would be enough to make her father feel somewhat guilty and leave her alone. Finishing with one last dramatic statement, she said, "I just want to have some time to myself."

But before Sadie could turn to leave and march

toward her bedroom, Jacob pulled himself to his feet. Staring right at his daughter, he asked, "Time to yourself—or time with Jensen Girod?"

The question turned her blood instantly to ice. Frowning, she realized that she hadn't even had time to prepare herself for his question, and her face surely betrayed the truth.

"Don't lie to me, *Dochder*!" Jacob exclaimed. "Levi Hostetler saw you riding to town with Jensen yesterday afternoon. He told me, but I decided to just let it be. I had hoped that maybe your ride with Aaron last night was a sign that something *gut* was happening, and I chose to leave it alone. But after tonight..." He shook his head sadly before looking up at her with accusatory eyes and asking, "You were with him, weren't you?"

Trying to lie her way out of the situation seemed futile. Nodding, Sadie chose to go with the truth and said, "*Ya, Daed*. I was."

While Jacob had known the truth, Sadie's confession made his face grow white. Pausing for a moment, he seemed to have to catch his breath before finally saying, "Sadie, I don't know what you're thinking. Jensen Girod is not a *gut bu*. You were too young to remember it, but he was a wild young *bu* who got into all kinds of mischief. He chose to leave the *Amisch* and in the process took several of the other young folk with him. He hates our ways, and he hates our faith. He's not someone you need to be around."

The words seemed bitter to her ears. Once again, she was lumped in with the Amish even though it was a lifestyle she had never chosen. Shaking her head, she let her tongue slip as she declared, "*Your* ways and *your* faith, *Daed*. Not mine. Do I need to remind you that I haven't been baptized yet? This is your *gmay*, not mine."

Jacob looked like she had driven a stake right through his heart. He seemed to stagger from the weight of it all, leaning his hand against the table before declaring, "You don't know what the *Englisch* life is like, Sadie!"

"*Nee*, I don't!" Sadie exclaimed, stepping forward so that only the table separated her from her father. Sparks of fire were shooting from her eyes as she narrowed them to stare at him and declare, "I never got to know...because of you and your overprotective ways. I never had the chance to do anything. All you did was tell me how evil the *Englisch* were...when there's nothing wrong with them at all." Stamping her foot against the hardwood floor, she confessed, "I was just a *kind* when I first looked at one of the forbidden magazines at the library. Rather than the life that you told me about, I saw people smiling and taking care of horses—not doing awful wrong things."

A volcano of lifelong pent up frustration erupted and was suddenly spewing forth from Sadie like searing molten lava.

"Sadie." Jacob reached up to rub the bridge of his nose as he tried to explain, "I was trying to protect you—to make sure that you didn't chase after a lifestyle that wasn't right for you. The modern world isn't where *Gott* put us!"

Before she could even think better of it, Sadie announced, "I'm not sure I even believe in *Gott, Daed*!"

Jacob sank down into his seat and covered his face at her brazen confession. In the aftermath of her announcement, Sadie wondered if she had made a mistake. Perhaps she had gone too far. She felt prompted to apologize to her father, yet she held herself back. Every word that she had said was true—there was no need to try and pretend otherwise.

After a moment, Jacob looked up at her with a face that looked both composed and serious. "Sadie, I can't force you to continue to stay *Amisch*.

But I will suggest that you look at the way that Jensen is being received by his *familye*. As someone who has not been baptized, you won't be shunned, but if you leave, you will still be an outcast. When you *kumm* to visit, people won't look at you the same way." Pausing as if about to deliver the weightiest factor to consider, Jacob declared, "And if you leave the *gmay*, you will not be allowed to visit your *maem's* grave any longer."

Now it was Sadie's turn to feel like she had been stabbed through the heart. How did her father know about her trips to the cemetery? And how dare he try to use them to guilt her into staying?

Reality began to slowly sink in as Sadie considered how much of her mother's memory she would truly have to leave behind if she went with Jensen.

"Just think about it, Sadie," Jacob pleaded. "Just go to bed and think about it."

Hurrying up the stairs, Sadie was glad that their conversation was over. She rushed to her room and slammed the door shut behind her. Leaning her back against it, she put her hands to her face to block the tears that were pouring down her cheeks.

Life was so unfair. What was she to do? Sadie had always considered leaving the Amish to be her goal in life, but her father had pointed out something important—leaving wouldn't come without its own share of sacrifices.

"I don't want to leave your memory, *Maem*!" Sadie whispered into the darkness of her room. "I just can't do that."

She wished that her mother could talk to her, giving her advice and telling her just what she wanted her to do. If only Sadie knew whether her mother would want her to stay there among the Amish or if she would encourage her to break free. Having her input would be what Sadie needed to make the right choice.

Reaching up to wipe her eyes, Sadie despised the tears that were still assailing her. It seemed that no matter what she did, her emotions were totally out of control and she was overwhelmed with a deep sense of pain and loss.

Grabbing the nearby hoe, Sadie was careful to get a weed without killing one of the small plants that grew next to it. Although it had been a day since she endured her midnight talk with her father, Sadie felt no better; in fact, she seemed to be somewhat worse.

Realizing all that was at stake to lose had burst the bubble of Sadie's enthusiasm for abandoning the Amish community and all that she knew. Ever since her father mentioned her being unable to visit her mother's grave, she had found herself suddenly torn.

The sound of an approaching buggy made her groan, and Sadie was almost afraid to look up. Fear that it might be her grandfather, she felt her heart fill with dread as she prepared herself for another stern lecture. Surely, if her father had heard about her visits with Jensen, then her grandfather would have as well. Nothing in the community was kept a secret from Bishop Kaufmann.

Daring to look up, Sadie let out a sigh of relief when she saw that it was Aaron Miller's buggy pulling to a stop in front of her house. At least Aaron had never been harsh with her. Even when she told him about her plans to eventually leave the Amish, he had been kind and sympathetic.

Putting her hoe aside, Sadie rubbed her hands on her apron and lifted one of them to wave.

Seeing her, Aaron mirrored her wave before stepping down from his buggy.

Making her way toward the front of the house, Sadie was somewhat glad that her father had left to run into town to pick up some feed. She didn't want him to see her spending time with Aaron and make comments about him courting her. While Aaron seemed to be a nice enough young man, Sadie certainly didn't feel like doing anything to pursue a relationship with anyone in their community. While she might have lost some of her fervor for leaving the Amish, she still didn't want to be tied down.

"*Gude daag*, Sadie!" Aaron called out. Lifting up a bag, he said, "I brought you something."

Making her way to his side, Sadie couldn't help but smile when she saw him pull a box full of pastries out of the bag.

"My *maem* made some cherry danishes last night," Aaron explained as he offered her the box. "Since you didn't want to *kumm* enjoy them fresh, I made sure to keep a few until today. They're her specialty. You have to try them."

Nodding appreciatively, Sadie motioned toward the porch and suggested, "How about we sit down, and I'll get some lemonade for us? I've been working out in the garden, and it would be nice to take a break."

Her words surprised even Sadie. She had been working so hard to stay distant toward Aaron, yet here she was inviting him to sit down and enjoy a snack with her. She had to admit that she didn't understand herself as she prepared the drinks and then went out to the porch where Aaron had already taken a seat in one of the handcrafted white rocking chairs.

Sitting down next to him, Sadie passed him a glass of lemonade before taking the box of pastries. Lifting one of the cherry danishes to her mouth, she bit into the flaky crust and closed her eyes in bliss. Letting out a moan, she exclaimed, "*Ach*! Your *maem* certainly does know how to bake!"

When she opened her eyes, Sadie saw that Aaron was smiling back at her. His smile quickly turned to a frown as he continued to look at her and asked, "Are you all right, Sadie? You don't seem at all like yourself today."

Taking another bite of the pastry, Sadie listened to a bird singing overhead as she tried to determine just how much to share with him. Shaking her head slowly, she admitted, "I'm afraid

I'm not all right. If I'm being honest, Aaron, the last few days have been rough." Tears began to cloud her vision as she said, "I met up with Jensen Girod—or Jensen Guthrie as he calls himself now."

Aaron raised an eyebrow, and an unpleasant look seemed to cross his face as he coolly replied, "I had heard that he was back in town visiting his *familye*."

"*Ya*," Sadie replied, rushing ahead with her story. "He was doing some work and stopped by to see them at the store—that's where we first met. We went on a few rides in his car together." Looking up as if she were seeking Aaron's approval, she admitted, "He asked me to go to New York City with him...and I agreed." Hurrying with her story, she shook her head as she said, "*Daed* found out and is so upset."

"I can imagine so," Aaron replied, his voice sounding strained and somewhat cold.

Narrowing her eyes, Sadie tried to understand Aaron's response. It seemed that his entire demeanor had changed in an instant. Cocking her head to one side, she asked, "Why? What's so awful about wanting to join the *Englisch*? What's wrong with wanting to have some modern conveniences?"

"Sadie"—Aaron reached up to run a hand through his hair, the same frustration that she had seen in her father's face evident in his own —"how on earth can you even ask that? Don't you understand at all? This is the path to the world and the evil that it contains! Why can't you see this?"

Rolling her eyes, Sadie asked, "What? *Gott's* going to send me to hell for what...using a washing machine? *Ach*, Aaron, you have to know how ridiculous that sounds!"

Aaron was getting more frustrated by the minute, and he was holding on to the arms of the rocking chair as if it might get away from him. "Sadie, it's not that. It's all that comes with that lifestyle. It's getting so caught up in possessions and the pursuit of money that one loses one's very soul. It's pushing *Gott* aside because you're so caught up in your fancy lifestyle."

Aaron's attitude was beginning to grate on Sadie's nerves, and she let out a bitter laugh as she asked, "Is that truly how you look at it?" Feeling a metallic taste rise up in her mouth, she declared, "You sound just like my *groossdaadi* and all the church leaders! Just trying to hold us back!"

"*Ya*!" Aaron returned, pulling himself to his feet, "*Ya*, I am trying to hold you back! Trying to hold you back from following the path of the devil! For goodness' sake, Sadie! How can you be so foolish about all this?"

Sadie had turned to Aaron because she had hoped for someone who would listen to her problems and help her. Instead, it appeared that she was destined just to get a younger version of Bishop Kauffman harassing her. Tears of bitter disappointment started to well up in her eyes as she grabbed the box of uneaten pastries and shoved them back toward Aaron. Pointing toward his buggy, she yelled, "I think I've had enough of your opinions for one day."

Not even giving him a chance to leave, Sadie turned on her heel and marched into her house, letting the door slam shut behind her. She had spent her entire life listening to men tell her what to do, and she certainly didn't intend on letting Aaron become yet another dictator on that long list of bossy rulers.

If that was what he considered to be friendship, then she was done with him completely!

Chapter Eleven

Aaron felt like he might be sick to his stomach as he drove his buggy down the road. He had tried so hard to be a kind friend to Sadie, going above and beyond to make her realize that she wasn't alone in the Amish community, yet in an instant, he had seen it all destroyed in front of him.

Jensen Girod.

The name made Aaron feel nauseous. He might have been young when Bridget left their family and the Amish community, but he could certainly remember that Jensen had played a role in her choice. He had been more than happy to help several of the Amish youth leave with him when he decided to turn his back on his faith. And now it seemed that Jensen was coming back to try to steal Sadie away as well. Just the thought of it made him so upset that he had spoken out of turn—and much too sharply for Sadie's liking, apparently.

Slowing his buggy, Aaron eyed the fork in the road. Going to the right would lead him back home to his parents' house, but turning to the left would take him to Grandpa Abe Miller's home and workshop.

If there was anyone who could help Aaron during this difficult time, it was his grandfather. Jerking on the reins, he guided the horses toward the left and down the short path that would take him toward the man from whose wisdom he longed to glean.

When Aaron pulled up next to his grandfather's shop, he smiled softly when he heard the sound of yodeling escaping from the open window. Abe Miller was known for being one of the best yodelers and singers in town, and Aaron had always known him to be one to sing as he worked.

Hopping down from the buggy seat, Aaron tied the reins to the hitching post and then made his way toward the front door. Pushing it open slowly, he soaked in the smell of fresh wood and called out, "*Groossdaadi*! It's me, Aaron!"

The yodeling stopped, and Abe Miller turned

around with a smile. Setting the wheel rung that he had been sanding to the side, he put his hands on his hips and said, "*Ach*! Another visit from my *kinnskind*? This truly is a pleasure! I tell you, these woman troubles may turn out to be more of a pleasure for me than I expected. At least they bring you around to see me."

Aaron had to chuckle to himself. His grandfather knew why he was back.

Stepping forward to lean his hand against the worktable, Aaron felt sawdust against his skin. "*Groossdaadi*, things have gone terribly wrong," he admitted with a shake of his head. "I followed your advice, and it seemed like Sadie and I were actually forming a friendship. I went on a walk with her and let Sadie talk, and then she really seemed to listen to me. Then we agreed to go on a buggy ride together. The buggy ride was a little bit more strained at first, but it turned out well. Then, today, I stopped by to see her with some of *Maem's* pastries."

Grandpa Abe grinned from ear to ear and jovially said, "Those pastries would make any day a *gut* one!"

Aaron didn't even feel light-hearted enough to laugh. Shaking his head glumly, he said, "*Nee.*

Not at all. She decided to talk again and tell me her troubles...only this time she shared some very troubling news. She's been seeing Jensen Girod while he's back in town."

At the mention of Jensen's name, Abe's smile dropped, and his entire face morphed into a frown. Crossing his arms against his chest, he muttered, "*Ach*, I had hoped that *bu* was gone for *gut*."

Letting out a sigh, Aaron admitted, "I hoped so too, but it's been going around the *gmay* that he was here doing some work and stopped by to see his *familye*. He's trying to convince his little *bruder* to leave the *Amisch*, but Seth won't pay him any attention. I guess when he happened to meet Sadie, he found the perfect person to lure away."

Abe bit down on his lip and stared off into space as if he were lost in thought. Shaking his head slowly, he reached up to tug at his beard as he said, "Jensen played a big role in getting Bridget to leave the *Amisch* back when you were still a *kind*."

While Aaron had known it to be true, hearing his grandfather admit it made it seem that much worse. If Jensen could lead Bridget astray, he would be able to convince Sadie to leave with him.

"What did you tell her?" Grandpa Abe asked.

Feeling embarrassed about his behavior,

Aaron rolled some sawdust between his thumb and finger before bluntly saying, "I was so upset that I acted cruelly toward her. I began to lecture her about why she needed to stay and told her I agreed with her *daed* and Bishop Kauffman. I told her that she was following the path of the devil and was foolish." Gritting his teeth , Aaron felt like he was enduring it all over again as he said, "I only made things worse in the end. Rather than listening to me, she seemed to be further convinced to leave by my words. She told me she'd had enough of my opinions and marched into the house. After that, I just left."

Grandpa Abe looked sick to his stomach as Aaron told his story, yet when it was finished, he let out a low chuckle. Whistling softly, he said, "*Ach*, Aaron. I think you still have quite a lot to learn about women." Raising a bushy eyebrow, he asked, "Did you ever stop to think that an attitude like that would just push Sadie farther away? She's feeling like the *gmay* holds nothing for her, and when you just meet her with more disapproval and condemnation, you're just proving to her that she's right."

Deep in his heart, Aaron knew that his grandfather was telling the truth, yet he had to ask, "Then what should I do, *Groossdaadi*? Was I just supposed to clap and say I was glad that she was leaving the faith? Pat her on the back and offer to help her pack? I don't know what to do!"

Stepping up next to him, Abe put a gentle but firm hand on Aaron's shoulder and gave it a squeeze as he announced, "*Nee*, nothing like that. But maybe you should consider telling Sadie just how much she matters to you. I can tell that you care deeply about her. Let her know that she has someone here in the *gmay* who cares for her—more than just caring about bossing her around."

The mere thought of admitting his feelings made Aaron's blood run hot, and he was sure that he was blushing bright red. Shaking his head, he squirmed away from his grandfather's grip and said, "*Ach*, I can't do that! That's just...that's not like me at all, *Groossdaadi*. I can't put my feelings out there like that."

Sighing, Grandpa scrunched his face into a frown as if he were in deep concentration. Then, as if one of the fancy *Englisch* light bulbs had gone off in his brain, he raised a finger and exclaimed, "I know just the thing!" Grinning like a mischievous little boy, he said, "Just because you can't tell her how you feel doesn't stop you from *showing* her how you feel. *Ya*, this is one situation that calls for a grand gesture!"

The gleam in his grandfather's eye made Aaron nervous. Eyeballing him suspiciously, he said, "What do you have up your sleeve?"

Reaching out to grab a hold of Aaron's arm, Abe Miller assured him, "Just what you might need to help you win Sadie Renno and let her know that she has some important reasons to stay."

Although he was a little frightened by his grandfather's suggestion, Aaron also found himself intrigued. Taking a seat by the workbench, he prepared himself to hear whatever the idea might be.

Lying in her bedroom, Sadie stared up at the ceiling and tried to imagine that she was somewhere else, anywhere else but in her home. The last twenty-four hours had been difficult, and at times she had wondered how she might endure them.

As if being chastised by her father and then Aaron wasn't bad enough, Grandfather Kauffman had come by the house that afternoon and gave her another severe tongue-lashing. He had heard about her time spent with Jensen and came to tell her about the folly of her ways. Bishop Kauffman had given her a long lecture about the truth of hell fire and how precariously close she was coming to its burning flames.

Shaking her head, Sadie turned over on her side and let out a deep breath as she reached up to wipe at yet more tears.

Of all the stern lectures that she had received, the visit from Aaron was the worst. Sadie had known that she couldn't share her heart with her father or grandfather, but she had at least hoped that Aaron might show some semblance of kindness and understanding. Unfortunately, she had been wrong. Aaron had simply tricked her, pretending to be kind until she revealed her deepest secrets; then he had pounced on her, stabbing a knife deep into her heart.

"I should never have thought he cared," Sadie whispered to herself as she studied the moonbeams dancing through the window and casting patterns on her quilted bedspread. "I should have known no one cares about me at all."

The only one who might have cared for Sadie

was her mother, and thanks to their foolish religious ways, she had been ripped from her life long before her time. At least Sadie wouldn't be there much longer. In a few weeks, Jensen would come get her, and then she would have the chance to actually experience the world, reveling in a place where she could find people who understood her and loved her rather than just trying to control her. Yet, as she thought about it, she reconsidered her father's words that leaving the Amish would block her from ever going to see her mother's grave. The idea of not being able to be near her mother broke her heart. It felt like Sadie was torn completely in two with her heart wondering which way to go. She only wished that her mother were there to help her make the right decision.

Chapter Twelve

Sadie's feet felt like she was dragging lead weights as she staggered toward the mailbox. She was forcing herself to take every step. Flipping the mailbox open, she frowned when she saw that the mail still hadn't arrived. She always got the mail at one o'clock in the afternoon. Sighing deeply, she wondered if her father might have picked it up on his way out of town.

Jacob had gone with Grandfather Kauffman to an auction in a nearby town, giving Sadie a strict warning that he expected her to still be there when he returned. It seemed that he was consumed with fear that she would run off any day now. But, truth be told, it was a valid concern. If Jensen were to show up on her doorstep that day, she would be ready to run off with him. On the other hand, thoughts about what she might lose if she did go with him plagued her mind.

The sound of an approaching buggy drew Sadie's attention; she looked up just in time to see Abe Miller headed her way. While she had always liked the cheerful older man, just knowing that he was Aaron's grandfather made her feel uncomfortable. Looking down at the ground, she wondered if he had already heard an earful about her from Aaron.

"Sadie?" Abe Miller sounded out of breath as he pulled his buggy to a stop next to her.

His exhausted voice elicited a surprised eyebrow raise from Sadie. She had often seen Abe go by when she was getting the mail, and he frequently stopped to greet her, but never had he seemed so tired or lackluster.

"*Gude mariye,* Mr. Miller," Sadie said as she reached a hand up to shield her eyes from the sun. "Are you all right this morning? You sound out of breath!"

Pushing his hat back on his forehead, Abe ran a hand through his hair and said, "*Ach,* I guess I'm just old. I just seem to be out of breath today." Squinting through one eye, he asked, "Is there any chance that you could help me get the buggy back home? If you'll help me, then I will make sure you get a ride back here."

Glancing toward the empty house, Sadie contemplated her decision. On the one hand, she certainly didn't feel like going anywhere with Aaron's grandfather, but on the other, she would feel awful if she refused and he didn't make it home unharmed!

Nodding, Sadie reached for the side of the buggy and pulled herself up onto the seat next to him. "I guess I can do that." Taking the reins from his hands, she explained, "My *daed* is gone until later this afternoon, so I don't suppose anyone will miss me."

Leaning back in the seat, Abe sucked in a deep breath of air and let it out slowly. "*Danki* for helping me, Sadie," he said with a smile as he took off his felt hat and used it to fan himself. "*Ach*, you young folk don't realize how hard it is getting old. You go from being able to do everything to becoming worn out doing practically nothing."

The comment made Sadie smile bitterly as she considered how ridiculous it truly was. Young folk getting to do everything was far from reality in her life!

Letting some of her thoughts slip past her lips, she admitted, "I think you must have forgotten what it's like to be young, Mr. Miller. Young folk don't get to do anything in our *Amisch gmay*—especially not young women. We're forced to listen to our elders and get bossed around until we finally get securely married, and then we get bossed by our *menner*."

Turning to look at her, Abe chuckled and admitted, "*Ach*, I guess you have a pretty *gut* idea of how it goes. But that's life, *Liewi*. We all have to submit to someone. Someone is going to be running your life, no matter what—either *Gott* or the devil. You just get to decide who it is that's in charge."

Suddenly feeling surprisingly at ease with the old man, Sadie looked right at him and asked, "And those who are *Amisch* are the only ones who are following the Lord? That's hard to imagine. If God exists, then I'm sure there are plenty of *Englischers* who let Him be a part of their lives too. Using cars and telephones doesn't mean that the devil is in charge of your life!"

As soon as her rant was over, Sadie braced herself for a tongue lashing. If she had delivered a speech like that to Grandfather Kauffman, there was no doubt she would've been severely chastised. But Abe didn't seem at all taken by surprise or mad at her; instead, he just nodded in agreement.

"*Ya, Liewi,* I'm sure that's true," he replied. "There are plenty of *gut, Gott*-fearing folk in the *Englisch* world. But what you have to worry about is where exactly the Lord is planting you. If *Gott* is calling you to the *Englisch* world, then by all means, follow Him. But just be sure it's actually the Lord doing the leading."

Sadie shifted in her seat, a physical manifestation of the discomfort caused by Abe's words. She didn't want to follow the devil, but she couldn't say that she wanted to follow God, either. She just wanted to follow her own ways. For once in her life, she wanted to be in charge. She wanted it so desperately that she wished there were more than the two explicit options.

Clicking her tongue, she urged the horses forward before asking, "Aaron told you about our fight yesterday, didn't he?"

Without hesitation, Abe nodded and said, "*Ya.* He came by my shop and told me. He knew that he'd spoken out of turn. He lost his elder *schweschder*, Bridget, to the *Englisch* when he was just a little *bu*. It's made things difficult for him and makes him sometimes sensitive to the thought of anyone leaving the *Amisch* way."

Sadie frowned as she considered it all from this perspective. She had always known that Bridget Miller left the Amish and to the best of her memory hadn't been seen or heard from in six years. Her heart softened a little as she realized Aaron likely didn't want the same for her.

"He's sorry for the way that he acted," Abe assured her. "Would you give him a second chance?"

Twisting her face into a frown, Sadie contemplated the question. She wasn't sure what to think. Finally, giving a shrug, she replied, "I suppose I would...if he were to ask me." Considering how shy and backwards Aaron could be, it was hard to imagine that he would ever think of making things right between them.

Sitting up straighter in the seat, Abe pointed toward an approaching drive and said, "There's my house and my workshop."

Noticing how much better he seemed to be feeling, Sadie guided the horses into the lane and parked in front of the workshop. "Is this *gut*, or do you want to go up to the house?"

Shrugging his shoulders, Abe donned his hat and said, "This will be fine. I'm feeling a lot better now. Besides, it looks like you might have someone waiting to talk to you."

Looking where Abe was motioning, Sadie felt her heart stop in her chest when she recognized Aaron standing near the workshop with a horse on either side of him, holding the reins of each horse in his hands.

Turning to look at Abe, Sadie's eyes narrowed as she watched the older man climb down from the buggy seat as spry as a teenager. So much for him being out of breath and fatigued!

Being set up didn't make Sadie feel good, yet at the same time, it warmed her heart a fraction to know that Aaron felt bad enough about their fight to try to make things right. Aaron Miller had always been a little on the shy side, and it was clearly difficult for him to go out of his way with such sweet gestures, so she was touched by his effort.

Climbing down from the buggy, Sadie walked the short distance to Aaron's side. Looking down at the ground, she announced, "Your *groossdaadi* says you want to talk."

Aaron nodded his head but then pointed at one of the horses as he explained, "I do…but I also know how much you like horses. How about we ride out toward the pond, and we can talk there."

A thrill of excitement surged through Sadie's body. She loved horseback riding, but it was something she was rarely allowed to do. Far too often her grandfather had stopped her, lecturing her about how unladylike it was to be seen galloping along with one's skirt pulled up past their knees.

Biting down on her lower lip, she finally gave a shy nod of her head and said, "*Ya*. I guess you've found my weakness. I can never say no to a horse ride."

Accepting the reins from Aaron, Sadie mounted the horse and reached down to softly pet its neck. Breathing in the scent of fresh horse sweat, she clicked her tongue and urged him forward as she called out, "I bet I'll beat you there!"

Aaron let out a laugh as he mounted his own horse and called out, "I bet you won't!"

Riding along through the bright spring afternoon, Sadie closed her eyes and let herself feel nothing but the wind in her face and the horse beneath her. Sunshine streamed down on her prayer *kapp*, and she felt as free as the breeze. In that moment, all of her worries about her future and her dreams of joining the *Englisch* melted away. All that mattered was the joy of the present.

∞∞∞

By the time they reached the pond, Sadie was out of breath and laughing so hard that her sides hurt. She couldn't remember a time when she had been more carefree and lighthearted. Slowing her horse to a stop, she couldn't help but smile at Aaron when he pulled his horse up beside her.

"I told you that I'd beat you," she said with a wide grin.

Aaron nodded his head and laughed along with her as he said, "I guess you were right."

Pointing toward an oak tree, he said, "Let's tie the horses over there and talk for a while."

Making their way toward the oak tree, Sadie felt like she was surely in a dream when she noticed a picnic blanket spread out on the ground beneath its shade with a wicker basket on top of it.

Dismounting her horse and hurrying to tie its reins to the tree, she turned to look at Aaron and asked, "What on earth?"

Aaron's face grew red as he admitted, "When I told my *groossdaadi* how things had gone between us yesterday, he offered to help me. He could tell I was upset at losing your friendship, and he helped me set all this up." Stepping up closer to her, Aaron looked down at the ground as he said, "Sadie, I really am sorry for how I acted yesterday. When you started talking about leaving the *Amisch*, I got scared. It reminded me so much of losing my *schweschder*, and I felt helpless. Rather than acting in kindness, I acted out of fear." Looking up to meet her eyes, he finished, "I should have never let myself behave in such a way. No matter what you decide, this is your life to live, and it's not my place to boss you around."

Unexpected tears pooled in Sadie's eyes at his raw and heartfelt confession. Never had anyone ever apologized to her before. In her entire life, she had been told what to do and lectured if she didn't obey the rules. Now Aaron Miller was offering her something different—he was offering her respect and the ability to make her own choices. How could she stay angry at him when he was trying so hard to be kind?

Nodding slowly, Sadie's voice came out as a whisper as she admitted, "I overreacted too. You sounded so much like my *groossdaadi* that I just started feeling trapped...and scared as well. I will forgive you if you will forgive me."

Aaron broke out into a broad smile, and he nodded as he said, "I think that's a deal that I can agree to! Now, let's see what *Groossmammi* fixed for us to snack on!"

Making her way toward the picnic basket, Sadie's heart felt lighter than ever before. And for the first time, she looked at Aaron and realized that their Amish community might actually have someone who she would not want to leave behind.

Chapter Thirteen

Sadie's mind kept returning to the picnic that she and Aaron had shared together the previous week as she tried to focus on tossing some feed to the chickens in their coop. While she had never intended for things to go so far, she and Aaron were spending more and more time together. It seemed almost every day that he came up with some reason to come by the house and see her.

And as much as Sadie hated to admit it, on the days when he didn't appear, it felt like her heart might break in two.

"At least it's put a smile on *Daed's* face," Sadie muttered to herself as she tossed some more food to the chickens. "And kept his nose out of my business."

Ever since she and Aaron started spending more time together, Jacob Renno had been less obsessed with monitoring her whereabouts. In fact, he had not mentioned Jensen once, and it was as if her indiscretions had been forgotten. He had done nothing toward trying to control her but appeared to have stepped back to let her do whatever she wanted with Aaron.

"That's just the way things go," Sadie said aloud as she considered the Amish ways. "You spend your entire life under the thumb of your *eldre*, only to have them ease up once they see you're about to be under the control of a *mann*."

Sadie knew that was what her father and grandfather were hoping would happen. They were hoping that she would become so enamored with Aaron that he would convince her to stay in the Amish community, get baptized, and lead a regular Amish life. The mere thought of it was enough to make her feel sick to her stomach.

Yet, Sadie also realized how close she was to giving in to their hopes. She was actually enjoying Aaron's company. Every day, she looked forward to spending time with him, and he had become her closest companion.

Sadie hadn't heard a word from Jensen since he left town, and she was starting to wonder if she ever would. Perhaps Jensen Girod-Guthrie had simply led her on. Maybe he had no intention of coming back for her. It might just be that she would truly transition into a romantic relationship with Aaron and eventually become one of the boring, constantly pregnant Amish housewives that were a part of their culture. The thought of it made Sadie grimace. She had to do something to keep that from happening!

"*Gude daag*, Sadie!" Aaron's voice drew her from her reverie, and Sadie felt her heart give an unexpected lurch when she saw his handsome face headed in her direction.

"*Gude daag*, Aaron," she called back. "What brings you out this way today?"

Leaning his arms against the wire siding of the chicken pen, Aaron shrugged and admitted, "Well, I invited you to *kumm* see our new filly after she was born, but you never took me up on that offer. Would you want to *kumm* out today?"

Looking around her, Sadie frowned as she considered how many chores she had yet to finish. Letting out a sigh, she said, "As much as I'd like to see the little foal, I still have a lot of chores left to do. I have to finish feeding the chickens, gather the eggs, and fill the cows' trough up with water."

Without missing a beat, Aaron reached for

the door to the chicken pen and swung it open. Stepping in beside her, he smiled as he declared, "I can help you do all that. If we're working together, you'll be done in plenty of time to go with me."

Grabbing a handful of chicken feed, Aaron began to spread it on the ground. Sadie's gaze lingered on him, watching as he worked to help her finish her chores quickly.

While Aaron might not be the type of person that Sadie had ever wanted to marry, she had to secretly admit that he was one of a kind, and in that moment, she was glad for the friendship they shared.

∞∞∞

Leading Sadie into his parents' horse barn, Aaron put his hands over her eyes and nudged her along in front of him. She giggled with every step that she took. When he nearly made her trip over a water bucket that was in the way, she laughed even harder.

Aaron told her that he wanted to keep her eyes covered so Sadie wouldn't catch a glimpse of the young filly until she could get a good look, but as he led her along, he had to admit to himself that it simply felt good to have his hands against her soft skin and feel her so close to him.

Stopping in front of one of the horse stalls, he pulled his hands back and said, "Here we are!"

There, within the pen, was their best horse, Maybella, and her tiny filly.

"*Ach*!" Sadie squealed as she bent over to get a better look at the foal. "I've never been this close to such a tiny horse before!" Sticking her hands in the pen, she urged the little filly to come toward her, coaxing it in sing-song tones.

Stepping back, Aaron was captivated as he watched Sadie working to lure the foal toward her outstretched hand. She looked like something out of a picture book. Not only was she beautiful, but Aaron also knew that she had changed in the time that they had been spending together.

While Aaron had been almost certain that their relationship was over after Sadie admitted that she had spent time with Jensen, it seemed that was only a bump in the road that had careened them toward better times. The fight that Aaron and Sadie had endured ultimately drew them closer together, and they were becoming the dearest of friends.

During their time together, Sadie had become so much more light-hearted and seemed almost at peace with herself and the Amish ways. Aaron could only hope that she would continue to let herself fall in love with their way of life—and hopefully Aaron himself. More than anything else, Aaron hoped and prayed that the Lord would keep Jensen far away!

∞∞∞

Cocking his head from one side to the other, Jensen Guthrie surveyed the building that was being constructed in front of him. Although he had only been gone from the project for a few weeks, he was proud to see how his plans were coming to fruition.

"This is going to be the biggest and most impressive nightclub in this area!" the contractor, Randy, announced as he stepped up to Jensen and gave him a slap on the shoulder. "And it's mainly thanks to your design."

Smiling smugly, Jensen replied, "Well, I think your team is making it come to life, but I won't turn down the compliment." Pushing his sunglasses up on his forehead, he added, "They don't call me the best in the Big Apple for nothing. Besides"—he nodded toward the building —"there's something terribly appealing about bringing a house of iniquity to my old home state."

Randy regarded him in confusion, but Jensen didn't feel like explaining. Instead, he just shook his head and said, "Let's wrap up the last few details, and then I'll be on my way."

Jensen didn't have time to explain how much satisfaction he derived from being involved in constructing buildings that went against his strict upbringing in their purpose. He could clearly remember his mother's horror when they had passed a nightclub once while traveling to a horse show in an *Englisch* driver's van. She had slung her hands over his eyes to try to keep him from seeing the scantily clad women lining the streets.

Now Jensen had the opportunity to aid in bringing one even closer to his old hometown. Finishing up his part of the project, Jensen assured Randy that he would be back once it was completed so that they could have a celebratory drink together. Then he hurried toward his waiting sports car. He still had someone he needed to see while he was in the area.

Sadie Renno—a sad Amish girl who needed someone to show her the path to freedom.

Jensen definitely didn't plan to give up on his opportunity to rip yet another Amish youth away from the fold. Smiling to himself, he chuckled as he fastened his seatbelt.

Sadie was a miserable, lonely girl with nothing to hold her to the Amish community. She was also pretty good looking. Once she was out of that plain Amish garb, Jensen might actually be interested in getting to know her a little better. Of course, he would never actually date her, but she might be a good girl to have on the side. After all, the Amish girls were known for trying to please, and Jensen might use that to his advantage when he was bored. In return, he would help Sadie adjust to the modern world.

In fact, if Jensen was lucky, he might just use her for a quick hook-up that very night. She had seemed pretty anxious to do anything to make him happy. Perhaps he could invite her to his hotel room where they could learn more about each other. Sadie Renno was putty in Jensen's hands—and he couldn't wait to mold her into whatever he wanted her to become. Putting his car into drive, he turned his vehicle back toward Morrissey

County and the beautiful Amish girl who waited for him there.

Chapter Fourteen

"*Danki* for the fun afternoon," Sadie announced as Aaron stopped his buggy outside her house. "I truly did enjoy seeing the little filly. You have some beautiful horses." Feeling a surge of emotion rise in her throat, she added, "Someday, I hope that I get to have twice that many horses, all of my own."

Aaron smiled back at her and said with sincerity, "You will."

Somehow, his words felt like they were a promise…a promise that Sadie wanted to cling onto. Looking into Aaron's green eyes, he had a sort of softness to them that she treasured, and she almost hated to be parted from him.

Making herself climb down from the buggy seat, she forced herself to remain in reality as she said, "I'd better get in here and see what I can do about getting something cooked for supper. *Daed* will be getting in from the fields here soon."

Saying a quick goodbye, Sadie hurried into the house. She shut the door behind her and leaned her back against it, trying to collect her good sense. Her mind seemed to be in a jumble where Aaron was concerned, and as much as she wanted to stay her course and keep her plans to leave the Amish community, he was making it difficult. All the days that they had spent together and all his attempts to make things pleasant for her had slowly started to chip away at Sadie's tough heart.

Closing her eyes, she whispered, "What do I do, *Maem*? How I wish you were here to give me some advice!" Pain pierced her heart as she considered how much she ached for the mother she had never known. She needed someone who could come alongside her, giving her direction and guidance. But the Amish faith had torn that away from her. It was their ignorant community that had decided her mother should give birth with only the help of a midwife—and that decision had cost her life.

Forcing herself to stop thinking about it, Sadie pulled herself to her feet and started toward the kitchen. Her father had left a note on the table that read, "I had to go help *Groossdaadi* do something in town. I will pick up pizza on the way home."

Running her finger along the note, Sadie shrugged and muttered, “That might not be the worst thing since we’re a little short on groceries.” Squaring her shoulders, she determined now would be as good a time as any to make a quick trip to the local store. The Girods’ store would surely be open by now and would be the perfect place to grab a few items needed to make fresh bread for the rest of the week.

∞∞∞

Guiding his buggy down the road, Aaron felt like he was meandering more than actually trying to get to a destination. After taking Sadie home, he had stopped by his grandfather’s workshop to have a quick chat and was now headed back home. The spring afternoon was beautiful, without a cloud to mar the clear blue sky. Aaron’s heart felt like it was equally as light and airy as the day. It was finally starting to feel like things were headed in the right direction with Sadie. She was starting to enjoy life there amongst her people—Aaron could feel it. She seemed to have developed a new sort of cheerfulness and lightheartedness, and Aaron hadn't heard her voice a complaint about the Amish community in days.

Perhaps now that Jensen Girod-Guthrie was out of the picture, she would finally be able to open her heart up to a life of satisfaction there amongst those of her faith.

Closing his eyes momentarily, Aaron whispered a silent prayer, "Please, *Gott*, let it be so. Let Sadie *kumm* to the point where she does appreciate and love this *gmay* and the life that she has laid out in front of her."

Opening his eyes, Aaron saw a black sports car headed in his direction. Aaron slowed his buggy and moved it to the side of the road so that the car could pass without slowing down. To his total shock, the car slowed down regardless, reducing to a crawl and stopping once it reached the buggy. Pulling on the reins, Aaron stopped his horse completely and waited to see what the driver might want. He must be a lost outsider trying to travel the country roads.

The tinted window rolled down to reveal a young man in his mid-twenties with short dark hair and a pair of sunglasses. Not even pushing the glasses back, the *Englischer* turned his attention to Aaron and asked, "Hey, do you know Sadie Renno?"

The question made Aaron's heart stop short. He squinted against the low sun so that he could see better. Surely this wasn't...Jensen Girod. Aaron hadn't seen him since he was just a little boy, Jensen being several years his senior. But Aaron was almost certain that this was indeed Jensen.

Swallowing hard around the lump that was rising in his throat, Aaron jutted out his bottom jaw and tried to make sense of what his archenemy was asking.

"Do you know Sadie Renno?" Jensen repeated, reaching up to push his glasses back on his head. Before Aaron could answer, he plowed ahead to explain, "I went by her house, but no one was home. Do you know what's going on? I need to know if she'll be back soon because I have to get back to town."

Aaron despised deceitfulness, yet in that moment, fibbing seemed the lesser of the two evils. "I'm sorry," he replied as he scratched his forehead and looked down at his hands, "Sadie and her *daed* had to travel out of state to go visit a sick relative. They won't be back until next week."

Jensen let out a low curse and exclaimed, "That's no good! I have to be back in the Big Apple tomorrow afternoon." Cursing again, he shook his head and gave a nod. "Thanks." With that, he rolled up his window and shifted the car into drive, practically roaring away from the place where he had stopped only seconds earlier.

Aaron's mare spooked and reared up on its hind legs, but he hurried to calm her down. Rushing to get her settled, he soothed, "Whoa, Ginger. Whoa."

It felt like all the peace and calm of the afternoon had been completely wiped away, replaced by confusion and distrust. All the confidence that Aaron had started to gather about Sadie had suddenly evaporated. He knew that it was wrong to lie, yet in that moment, he didn't regret lying to Jensen. If anything would get rid of the main threat to Aaron's happiness, he was ready to do whatever it took. Holding his breath, he could only hope that Jensen would truly buy the lie that he had told and would head off to New York City, never to think of Sadie again.

Swinging the bag of groceries at her side, Sadie smiled as she made her way back home.

Evening was starting to close in, yet the day still held beauty. Closing her eyes as she walked, Sadie breathed in the fresh scent of the spring flowers swaying in the breeze alongside the road.

Although it was surely five o'clock by now, she figured she would have plenty of time to get home and start on some bread before her father got back home. She looked forward to sharing pizza with him, and as ridiculous as it seemed, she was in such good spirits that she didn't think she would mind Grandfather Kauffman staying to eat with them!

Sadie had enjoyed such a delightful day with Aaron Miller and could hardly wait to spend more time with him the next afternoon. Looking up, she felt her heart skip a beat in her chest when she spotted a familiar car making its way up the road. Driving directly toward her, the black sports car looked just like the one that belonged to Jensen Guthrie.

Could it be that Jensen had actually returned? It had been so long that Sadie had all but given up on him. The car slowed down and pulled to a stop right next to her. The driver's window rolled down to reveal the familiar face of Jensen, sunglasses and all.

"Jensen!" Sadie breathed his name in shock and shook her head as she admitted, "*Ach*! I figured you'd forgotten me by now."

Smirking back at her, Jensen pushed the sunglasses up on his forehead and said, "Scratch that idea out of your mind—I could never forget a face as pretty as yours." Motioning toward the passenger seat, he added, "Get in. We've got a lot of catching up to do!"

Sadie had been so anxious to see Jensen again, yet as she climbed into his passenger seat, she felt a sinking feeling in the pit of her stomach. Rather than being excited, she suddenly felt a wave of uncertainty overwhelm her. Her time with Aaron had done something to her that changed her, making her wonder how much she actually wanted to leave with Jensen.

"How about we go to town and grab a burger?" Jensen suggested.

Shrugging, Sadie wished that she felt more enthusiastic as she said, "That would be nice."

Turning to direct his car back toward town, Jensen smiled and reached across to put a hand on hers as he said, "I thought about you a lot while I was back in New York City. In fact, you were all I thought about. It was like I had a picture of you constantly playing through my mind."

While his words were sweet and endearing, they didn't do the same thing to Sadie that they would have during their first visit. Swallowing hard, she forced herself to smile as she said, "Well, you get to see the real version of me now." Trying to turn his attention toward other things, she asked, "How was life back in New York City?"

Jensen let out a deep breath and shook his head. "It was busy. If there's one way to describe the Big Apple, that's it: busy." He laughed and said, "Big, busy, and noisy. When you're walking along the streets of New York City, you can stop, and it feels like you're in a sea of people. And they all just keep walking around you, paying no attention to you at all. Some of them are cursing and some of them are fighting. It's like being an ant in a huge world. And everyone is just fighting to be the biggest ant."

Biting down on her lip, Sadie couldn't help but feel somewhat disappointed in his description of the *Englisch* life. That didn't sound a thing like the picture she had seen in the magazine!

"Don't worry," Jensen assured her as he gave her hand a squeeze. "Pretty soon, you'll get to see it for yourself. You'll be right there in the midst of the crowd."

Glancing out the window, Sadie watched as the trees and flowers went whizzing past. What would a concrete world be like with people who didn't care about each other? Could that lifestyle ever actually fill her heart with what had always been missing?

"I'm going back to New York tomorrow," Jensen told her. "I want you to come with me. Do you still want to?" Not even giving her a chance to answer, he plowed ahead to suggest, "Why don't you come meet me at my hotel room tonight, and we can talk it all over? We can leave together from there."

Meet at the hotel room? Sadie felt herself instantly bristle, and Jensen must have noticed. Laughing nervously, he added, "Don't read more into that than I meant. I wouldn't do anything to hurt you or disrespect you."

Before she could say anything or let her mind linger on his words, he rushed ahead to declare, "I sure was glad to find you. I went by your house, but no one was there. Then I met some Amish guy on the road, and he said you had traveled out of state for a week. I figured I'd missed my chance to see you."

Stiffening in her seat, Sadie held up a hand to stop him from saying anything else. Turning to look at him, she asked, "What did you say? Who told you that?"

Shrugging, Jensen said, "I didn't recognize him. Some young guy. Probably around your age... driving a buggy alone. Curly dark hair...green eyes."

Aaron Miller.

Sadie felt her blood start to boil in her veins. How dare he do this to her? How dare he try to keep her apart from Jensen? Aaron had told her that he wouldn't try to control her, yet he had done just that! He was just like all the other Amish men in her life—controlling and trying to hold her down. No one told the truth; everyone just told lies! How could a lifestyle of supposed faith be full of so much deception?

Sucking in a deep breath of air, she exhaled slowly and said, "Jensen, I'm going to have to skip out on that trip to the restaurant. I have some business to take care of. How about I call you from the phone shanty later tonight?"

Sadie was so mad that she could hardly even hear his reply. She got out of the car as quickly as possible and started marching toward the Miller house. Aaron would be confronted for what he had done!

Chapter Fifteen

Making her way toward Aaron Miller's house, Sadie became cognizant of the fact that her legs were burning from walking so quickly and so far. The day had been full of exercise, more than she usually got, yet she was so mad that she hardly cared. How dare Aaron betray her once again? She had put everything out on the line to believe in him and trust him, yet this was how he repaid her?

While Jensen's description of life in New York City had soured her idea of the *Englisch* lifestyle, she wasn't sure that she wanted to stay in Morrissey County either. She knew without a doubt that she wanted nothing else to do with Aaron. Even if she were to stay Amish, she promised herself that she would have nothing more to do with him and would never speak to him again. All she needed to do was give him one last piece of her mind. He needed to know just what she thought of him and to feel some sense of guilt for being just like everyone else in their community.

Looking toward the Miller horse barn, Sadie noted that the wooden doors were pushed open, and she could easily see the form of someone working inside. Even from a distance, she quickly recognized it as Aaron.

"*Gude daag,* Sadie!" one of Aaron's little brothers called out from the back yard, where the rest of the family was working in the garden.

Sadie didn't even return his greeting; instead, she just marched resolutely to the barn. Stepping up to the barn door, she watched as Aaron scooped up some loose straw with a pitchfork. Her heart broke as she considered all that he had done for her and the way that he had betrayed her. Realizing that she could hardly even say his name, Sadie cleared her throat loudly. Aaron dropped the pitchfork and turned around in surprise, his look turning from shock to joy and then to concern. Taking a step toward her, he asked, "Sadie, are you all right?"

Clearing her throat again, Sadie shook her head and said, "*Nee,* I'm not all right. I'm not all right at all." Putting a hand on her hip, she bluntly asked, "Did you tell Jensen that I was on a trip? Did you lie so that he couldn't see me?"

Aaron opened his mouth, but nothing came out—the look on his face said it all.

Shaking her head in disgust, Sadie laughed bitterly and muttered, "Why am I not surprised? You turned out like everyone else...yet it still hurts. I don't want to see you ever again, Aaron. Our friendship is over." She turned and started toward the barn door, but with every step she took, another barrage of thoughts swirled through her mind.

Turning back around, she took another step toward him and narrowed her blue eyes as she pointed a finger at him and declared, "You acted like you cared about me. You acted like my opinion mattered and that you respected me. What a joke! You are a liar through and through. You try to pretend to be so pious and righteous, yet you are nothing but a dirty fibber."

Sucking in a deep breath, she started toward the door, only to turn back around and yell, "You are going to be just like my *daed* and *groossdaadi*! You are going to be a stubborn, mean old *mann* who will be a control freak. If you ever get a *fraa*, then I pity her because you will be brutal and rule her with an iron fist."

Determining that she was finished with Aaron, Sadie felt hot tears start to rise from deep within her. She just wanted to turn as quickly as she could and run back home, but before she could even start to take a step toward the door, Aaron stepped up next to her. He reached out and grabbed her arm, holding it firmly and yet gently in his grasp.

"Sadie!" The way he said her name made her stop, and she looked up into his eyes that seemed overwhelmed with pain and frustration. "Sadie, stop! I never meant to hurt you. I never meant to control you at all. I didn't even mean to lie. I just knew that I had to say something to get Jensen to leave you alone." Shaking his head, he used his free hand to reach up and rub his hand through his hair as he declared, "Don't you understand? You're more than just a friend to me—you mean everything to me! You are the sweetest, dearest, best *maedel* that I could ever dream of finding. You are irreplaceable! And I love you!"

Sadie took a step back in surprise, pulling her arm away from his grasp. "You what?" she repeated, her eyes growing large.

“I love you!” Aaron repeated, his voice little more than a whisper.

All of Sadie’s life, she had longed for someone who would speak to her as Aaron just did. While Jensen’s words had been full of compliments, there was something about Aaron’s that seemed much more genuine. His confession made Sadie’s heart stop in her chest, and she wondered how to even accept it.

Suddenly, Sadie felt an overwhelming urge to get away. Turning on her heel, she pushed the barn door open and ran out into the sunshine. She had to get away and get her head back on straight. She couldn’t let her heart take her down this path!

Watching Sadie run away from him, Aaron’s heart squeezed and ached deep in his chest. What on earth had just happened? He had bared his soul to her, yet to his horror, it seemed to push her even farther away. What if he had lost her completely?

Dropping his head and closing his eyes, Aaron whispered a prayer, “Why *Gott*? Why have You allowed things to turn out this way? I tried to share my heart with Sadie, but that only seemed to make things worse. Why have You led me down this path?"

Even as he prayed, Aaron realized that the Lord wasn't done working on Sadie yet. Perhaps Aaron had been so busy focusing on winning her heart for himself that he had forgotten that he needed to allow the Lord a chance to win her heart for Himself. After all, Aaron's relationship with her was important, but the Lord's relationship with her was eternal. This was one situation that Aaron was simply going to have to leave in the Lord's hands.

"But that won't keep me from trying to protect her from afar," Aaron whispered to himself. While he couldn't make up Sadie's mind for her, he could do whatever it took to ensure that she didn't get harmed in the process.

The sound of an approaching car made Aaron stand up straighter and peer out the open barn door. Their *Englisch* driver, Ben Wilson, had just returned, bringing his mother home from a shopping expedition in town.

Forcing himself not to give in to the threatening tears, Aaron was determined to go help her unload the groceries, silently praying that the Lord would make it clear to him how to protect dear Sadie from a distance.

∞∞∞

Standing in the phone shanty, Sadie pulled the phone away from her ear and hung it up on the receiver. The small phone shanty was the place where many Amish in the community went to book rides with *Englisch* drivers.

Looking down at the suitcase that she had set down at her feet, Sadie shook her head slowly. She was planning another night of sneaking away from home without her father's knowledge—but this time, it was for good.

Talking to Aaron had only confused Sadie more and proven to her that she needed to get away from the community. When he had declared his love for her, it had almost convinced her to stay and remain Amish. She couldn't let herself go down that road!

Being Amish was the last thing that Sadie wanted! She didn't want to give up her dreams of the *Englisch* lifestyle—the dreams that she had held so dear to her heart since she was just a little girl. If she stayed any longer, that was exactly what she would end up doing.

Ben Wilson had promised Sadie that he could pick her up at the phone shanty in just a few minutes. He was already out and about after having dropped someone else off. Once he arrived, he would be taking her into town to the hotel.

Pressing her lips together, Sadie wondered exactly what the future might hold. Jensen was an extraordinary young man—just the type she should be proud to have giving her some attention, yet there was something hollow about him. Pushing the thought away, she convinced herself that she was doing the right thing. Jensen was the man she needed to turn to if she wanted a life that was anything other than being barefoot and pregnant for the rest of her existence.

Wonder if Daed has returned home and found my note yet. The thought made Sadie sick to her stomach. She hated the idea of her father coming back home and seeing that his daughter had left, but in that moment, she tried to pretend that she didn't care. After all, soon she would be starting a new life, and her father would be a piece of the past.

The sound of an approaching vehicle made her

stand to attention, and she hurried to open the door to the shanty and step out into the night. Darkness had finally wrapped Morrissey in its grip, and the overcast sky threatened to unleash rain, which was fitting for Sadie's new beginning. That would be the night she would say goodbye to the past and hello to the future.

Chapter Sixteen

Stepping into the only hotel in town, Sadie turned and watched out the double glass doors as Ben's car drove out of view. An older man, Ben Wilson asked few questions and always seemed to be anxious to get to his next job. While Sadie was glad that he didn't like to pry, there had been something almost sad about his hurrying off when she knew that it might be the last time she would ever see him.

After making her way to the reception desk, Sadie rang a small bell that was set on it and waited for someone to appear. Within a few seconds, a young attendant had stepped out from the back, a smile plastered on her face.

"Welcome to Guest Suites!" she said in a sing-song voice. "How can I help you?"

Biting down on her lower lip, Sadie said, "I need to speak to one of your guests. His name is

Jensen Guthrie."

The attendant turned to her computer screen and began to type, her face turning into a frown as she looked up to meet Sadie's eyes and said, "I'm sorry, but there's no Jensen Guthrie staying here."

Sadie's heart constricted in panic. "How about Jensen Girod?"

A few seconds more, and the attendant was shaking her head again. "I'm sorry, but he's not here. Maybe he's gone to a nearby town?"

The suggestion made Sadie's heart flutter in fear. What would she do if Jensen was gone? Nodding slowly, she asked, "Do you have a telephone that I can use?"

The attendant shook her head and gave a sad smile as she said, "No, only guests can use our phones. But if you'd like, there's a payphone right outside at the edge of the parking lot."

Sadie muttered a thanks. Stepping back out into the night, she pulled her black jacket a little tighter against her as a chilly wind blew through her bones. The spring night had begun to feel like winter, and judging by the wet feeling in the air, it would likely start pouring at any second.

After finding the small phone booth, Sadie stepped inside and dug around in her dress pocket until she located several coins. She had already given Ben Wilson almost all of her money. She could only hope that Jensen would show up to help her—surely he wouldn't have gone back to New York without telling her!

Pulling out his business card along with the money, Sadie wished that she had just called Jensen first. Dialing the number, she waited as it rang again and again. Finally, just when she was about to give up hope, there was a click on the other end, and Jensen's familiar deep voice called out, "Jensen Guthrie! How can I help you?"

Letting out a sigh of relief, she pulled the phone closer to her mouth as she tried to talk around the lump that was quickly forming in her throat. "Jensen, it's me...it's Sadie. I came to the hotel in town, and you weren't here..." Her voice trailed off.

"You did what?" Jensen asked. "What do you mean? I thought you couldn't meet me because you had business to take care of?"

Shaking her head as if he could see her, she tried to explain, "I had a change of plans. I'm here in town trying to find you, but they say you're not at the hotel."

"No, I'm not," Jensen replied, his tone

sounding almost irritated. "I'm at a nearby town—closer to the building I've been working on."

"Can you come get me?" Sadie pleaded as she looked out into the drizzle that was now falling from the sky.

In the background, Sadie could hear something that sounded like a woman's voice giggling. Her blood instantly ran cold. Where exactly was Jensen?

"No, I can't tonight," Jensen said, his irritation only growing, "I'm a little busy right now."

"Jensen…come on!" a woman's voice teased from the other end of the line. "Come over here…I *need* you!"

Sadie's chin began to quiver as she realized exactly what was going on. "Who is that?" she managed to ask around the lump in her throat.

"That was no one," Jensen hurried to reply. "It's my mother. She's here with me."

Sadie knew the truth. There was no chance that Jensen's Amish mother would possibly be at the hotel with him, and even if she were, she certainly wouldn't use that tone of voice with him!

Jensen was with another woman. Despite all his talk of only having eyes for Sadie, he had managed to find someone else to entertain him for the night. Not even trying to argue with him, Sadie lifted the phone and slammed it back down on its base. Things between her and Jensen were over.

The reality of what she had just lost hit Sadie like a ton of bricks. While she had never been sure of Jensen, she never would have guessed that he was so capable of leading her on. Tears began to pour down her cheeks. Looking out into the rain, she realized that she had nowhere left to turn. She didn't have any money left to pay a driver to come pick her up, and she had no money to pay for a room. She could try to walk home, but it seemed that she had burned every bridge in Morrissey County, so what was the point of returning? Sinking down so that she was crouched on the ground inside the tiny phone booth, she began to sob.

"*Gott*!" she cried out a prayer. "Where am I supposed to turn now? What am I supposed to do?"

For the first time in her life, Sadie realized that it was the Lord that she was praying to instead of trying to talk to her dead mother. All these years of trying to talk to her mother had gotten her nowhere; it had only given her more pain. Perhaps it was time to turn her heart over to the only One who could truly give her guidance.

"I don't know what to do, *Gott*!" she sobbed, tears beginning to roll down her cheeks. "I don't know where to go. I don't know what kind of life to live! Please, show me! I want to live the life You want for me!"

Looking up, Sadie let out a scream at the sight of the silhouette of a man standing outside of the phone booth. In the darkness of the night, he seemed foreboding and frightening. Pulling herself to her feet, she grabbed the telephone and held it in her hands, prepared to use it if she had to fight him.

The glass door of the phone booth opened just as the clouds moved away, and to her surprise, she found herself staring right into the green eyes of Aaron Miller.

"Listen, Sadie!" Aaron exclaimed, holding up his hands as if to plead his innocence. "I'm sorry for showing up like this, but I had to make sure that you were okay."

Dropping the phone and letting it swing from the cord, Sadie stepped out of the booth and threw her arms around Aaron, pulling him against her in a hug. When it had felt like everything in the world was against her, God had sent Aaron to her aid.

"Don't be sorry!" Sadie exclaimed as she cried into his shoulder. "*Danki* for being here... especially after I was so harsh to you. How did you know where to find me?"

Aaron shrugged and admitted, "Ben Wilson was at our house bringing my *Maem* home when you called. His phone is turned up so loud I could overhear every word." Pushing Sadie back so that he could look in her eyes, Aaron said, "Sadie, I'm not going to try to control your life, and I'm not going to try to force you to stay *Amisch*...but I did want to make sure that you would be safe while you made your choice. If you want me to leave, then I'll understand."

Reaching up to wipe at her eyes, Sadie shook her head and whispered, "*Nee*, I don't want you to leave...not unless you're ready to take me with you." Confidence about her choice filled her heart as she said, "I don't have any choice left to make. Your *groossdaadi* was right—we're either being led down the right path by the Lord, or we're being led astray by Satan. Tonight, I put my future in the hands of *Gott*."

Aaron's face broke out in a broad grin, and he pulled Sadie back toward him, wrapping her in a hug that was warm enough to protect her from the cold night. "I don't know what I would have done if you had really left," Aaron admitted, and pulling back to look into her eyes, he put his thumb against her chin as he added, "because I couldn't imagine my life without you."

Suddenly realizing what was waiting for her at home, Sadie let out a groan and said, "*Ach*, I don't know how I will ever face my *daed* or *groossdaadi*!"

Reaching down to take her hand in his own, Aaron smiled and whispered, "Don't worry—you won't have to face them alone."

For the first time in her life, Sadie realized how true that those words really were. She didn't have to face anything without someone by her side—Aaron would be with her, and even better than that, she knew that the Lord would always be with her as well. And how could anyone ask for a better life than that?

Epilogue

Sadie reached up to wipe a stray tear from her eye as she looked down at the plain gravestone. She didn't come to the cemetery much anymore, yet on this day it seemed appropriate. Biting down on her lip, she considered all that had happened over the past six months and just how much her life had changed. After her experience with Jensen and her choice to put her life in the hands of the Lord, she had seen a complete change in her circumstances.

Just as Sadie had expected, her father had been upset when she returned home, with Grandfather Kauffman being absolutely furious with her. They had done little to try to welcome her; instead, they poured shame down on her. Yet, through it all, Aaron had stood faithfully by her side. Every hole that had been in her heart felt like it had been filled, and it cemented her decision to remain Amish.

"I've spent my entire life wishing that you were here with me, *Maem*," Sadie whispered into the wind as she reached up to push some stray hair out of her face. "I now realize that I don't need your guidance. I depend on the Lord to guide me. I have confidence in the future and what it holds. But today, I do wish that you were here to see me marry the *mann* I love."

Sadie's heart felt like it was going to swell beyond its capabilities as she considered the fact that in just a few short hours she would gather with the rest of the community to tie her heart and future to that of Aaron Miller. Despite her lifelong desire not to live a life as an Amish woman, it seemed that was exactly where the Lord had put her—and Sadie was excited to see what the future might hold.

"Sadie!" the voice of Jacob Renno called out, and she turned to see her father headed in her direction.

Stepping up to her side, Jacob smiled as he said, "Something told me that I might find you here."

Nodding, Sadie reached out and took her father's hand in her own. Smiling, she said, "Once

I get married, I'll be too busy to make very many trips out here to see *Maem*. Aaron and I are going to work on starting our own horse farm, and he's anxious to get a *familye* started too. I just thought it would be nice to see her again."

Giving his daughter's hand a gentle squeeze, Jacob looked into her eyes and said, "She would be proud of you, Sadie. Your *maem* would truly be proud."

Tears started to well up in Sadie's eyes as she grasped the reality of what her father was saying. He had never been one to talk about her mother and had certainly never been one to tell Sadie what life choices might make his deceased wife happy. Leaning her head against his shoulder, Sadie stared down at the marker and closed her eyes.

Finally, she was at peace and excited about what the future might hold for her...right there in Morrissey County.

Find out more of what happens to the women of Morrissey County as they search for love and acceptance.

Sarah (The Amish of Morrissey County Prequel)

Morrissey County, 1979

Sarah Kauffman has always abided by the Ordnung, and not only because her father happens to be the town's bishop and would, she feels, disown her if she didn't. But when her mother passes away, she longs to escape the clutches of her father and run away to the Englisch world. When her father wants her to marry someone she doesn't love, Sarah becomes even more desperate to leave.

Jacob Renno, on the other hand, is happy with life on his farm. It keeps him so busy that the older bachelor has no time for love, but on lonely nights, he finds himself longing for a companion.

When Sarah and Jacob meet, there's an instant connection, but things get complicated. Jacob offers to help Sarah with her dilemma, but Bishop Kaufmann insists that she obey his wishes. Will Sarah run off to join the Englisch, or will the handsome farmer give her pause? Will her father disown her or give her his blessing?

Bridget (The Amish of Morrissey County Book Two)

Morrissey County, 2000

Bridget Miller, the sister of devout Amish community member Aaron Miller, returns from life amongst the Englisch to a guarded Aaron who isn't sure he can trust her and doesn't want her affecting his happy life. He is determined to protect his family from Bridget's influence.

Steven Smoker wants nothing more than to take over his father's farm. However, his father refuses to leave the farm to a bachelor. Steven must marry an Amish girl or forfeit the farm. He begins to lose hope since Bridget Miller, the only girl he's ever loved, left the Amish years ago.

Steven runs into Bridget unexpectedly and learns that she wishes to return to the Amish! Will Steven be able to accept and trust Bridget despite her past? Will others in the community welcome her or shun her?

Abigail (The Amish of Morrissey County Book Three)

Morrissey County, 1980

Jonas Smoker longs for a solitary life on his own farm. His widowed mother wants grandchildren, but he's bound and determined to live out his dream on his own.

Abigail Speicher has been distraught since her father's passing, and she wonders if finding a husband will turn her grief into joy. However, her latest prospect is more interested in himself than in her.

When Jonas travels out of town to purchase supplies from the Speicher's reputable farm supply store, he becomes smitten with Abigail. Love seems set to blossom between the pair, but Abigail's rejected suitor won't give her up so easily. He conspires with the bishop to turn the young couple against one another. Is Jonas doomed to being a life-long bachelor? Will Abigail ever be cherished?

Eliza (The Amish of Morrissey County Book Four)

Morrissey County, 2022

Eliza Miller is keen on the Englisch life. She got a job in a large real estate company and worked her way up to being the boss's secretary. The more she gets to know Englischers, the more she desires to break free of the shackles of her Amish community.

Andrew Blythe has built up and sold several businesses since he was in high school. Now, he's at the helm of a profitable real estate company.

Still, he wonders if there's more to life than making money.

Eliza takes Andrew to meet her Amish relatives, and he begins to imagine a different life for himself. However, when Bishop Kauffman discovers Andrew's hidden secret, he sets his sights on keeping his great-granddaughter from marrying Andrew. Will he succeed in meddling in his family's love affairs one last time? Or can Eliza and Andrew overcome the obstacles in their way and forge a new path?

Thank you, readers!

Thank you for reading this book. It is important to me to share my stories with you and that you enjoy them. May I ask a favor of you? If you enjoyed this book, would you please take a moment to leave a review on Amazon and/or Goodreads? Thank you for your support!

Also, each week, I send my readers updates about my life as well as information about my new releases, freebies, promos, and book recommendations. If you're interested in receiving my weekly newsletter, please go to newsletter.sylviaprice.com, and it will ask you for your email. As a thank-you, you will receive several FREE exclusive short stories that aren't available for purchase!

Blessings,
Sylvia

Books By This Author

The Origins Of Cardinal Hill (The Amish Of Cardinal Hill Prequel)

Available for FREE on Amazon

Two girls with a legacy to carry on. A third choosing to forge her own path.

Welcome to Cardinal Hill, Indiana! This quaint fictional town is home to Faith Hochstetler, Leah Bontrager, Iris Mast, their families, and their trades. Faith, Leah, and Iris are united in their shared passion for turning their hobbies within nature into profitable businesses...and finding love! Find out how it all begins in this short, free prequel!

Other books in this series:
The Beekeeper's Calendar: Faith's Story
The Soapmaker's Recipe: Leah's Story
The Herbalist's Remedy: Iris's Story

The Origins of Cardinal Hill is the prequel to the Amish of Cardinal Hill series. Each book is a stand-alone read, but to make the most of the series, you should consider reading them in order.

A Promised Tomorrow (The Yoder Family Saga Prequel)

Available for FREE on Amazon

The Yoder Family Saga follows widow Miriam Yoder and her four unmarried daughters, Megan, Rebecca, Josephine, and Lillian, as they discover God's plans for them and the hope He provides for a happy tomorrow.

The Yoder women struggle to survive after Jeremiah Yoder succumbs to a battle with cancer. The family risks losing their farm and their livelihood. They are desperate to find a way to keep going. Will Miriam and her daughters be able to work together to keep their family afloat? Will God pull through for them and provide for them in their time of need?

A Promised Tomorrow is the prequel to the Yoder Family Saga. Join the Yoder women through their journey of loss and hope for a better future. Each book is a stand-alone read, but to make the most of the series, you should consider reading them in order. Start reading this sweet Amish romance today that will take you on a rollercoaster of emotions as you're welcomed into the life of the Yoder family.

The Christmas Cards: An Amish Holiday Romance

Lucy Yoder is a young Amish widow who recently lost the love of her life, Albrecht. As Christmas approaches, she dreads what was once her favorite holiday, knowing that this Christmas was supposed to be the first one she and Albrecht shared together. Then, one December morning, Lucy discovers a Christmas card from an anonymous sender on her doorstep. Lucy receives more cards, all personal, all tender, all comforting. Who in the shadows is thinking of her at Christmas?

Andy Peachey was born with a rare genetic disorder. Coming to grips with his predicament makes him feel a profound connection to Lucy Yoder. Seeking meaning in life, he uses his talents to give Christmas cheer. Will Andy's efforts touch Lucy's heart and allow her to smile again? Or will Lucy, herself, get in his way?

The Christmas Cards is a story of loss and love and the ability to find yourself again in someone else.

The Christmas Arrival: An Amish Holiday Romance

Rachel Lapp is a young Amish woman who is the daughter of the community's bishop. She is in the midst of planning the annual Christmas Nativity play when newcomer Noah Miller arrives in town to spend Christmas with his cousins. Encouraged by her father to welcome the new arrival, Rachel asks Noah to be a part of the Nativity.

Despite Rachel's engagement to Samuel King, a local farmer, she finds herself irrevocably drawn to Noah and his carefree spirit. Reserved and slightly shy, Noah is hesitant to get involved in the play, but an unlikely friendship begins to develop between Rachel and Noah, bringing with it unexpected problems, including a seemingly harmless prank with life-threatening consequences that require a Christmas miracle.

Will Rachel honor her commitment to Samuel, or will Noah win her affections?

Join these characters on what is sure to be a heartwarming holiday adventure! Instead of waiting for each part to be released, enjoy the entire Christmas Arrival series at once!

Amish Love Through The Seasons (The Complete Series)

Featuring many of the beloved characters from Sylvia Price's bestseller, The Christmas Arrival, as well as a new cast of characters, Amish Love Through the Seasons centers around a group of teenagers as they find friendship, love, and hope in the midst of trials. ***This special boxed set includes the entire series, plus a bonus companion story, "Hope for Hannah's Love."***

Tragedy strikes a small Amish community outside of Erie, Pennsylvania when Isaiah Fisher, a widower and father of three, is involved in a serious accident. When his family is left scrambling to pick up the pieces, the community unites to help the single father, but the hospital bills keep piling up. How will the family manage?

Mary Lapp, a youth in the community, decides to take up Isaiah's cause. She enlists the help of other teenagers to plant a garden and sell the produce. While tending to the garden, new relationships develop, but old ones are torn apart. With tensions mounting, will the youth get past their disagreements in order to reconcile and produce fruit? Will they each find love? Join them on their adventure through the seasons!

Included in this set are all the popular titles:
Seeds of Spring Love
Sprouts of Summer Love
Fruits of Fall Love
Waiting for Winter Love
"Hope for Hannah's Love" (a bonus companion short story)

Jonah's Redemption (Book 1)

Available for FREE on Amazon

Jonah has lost his community, and he's struggling to get by in the English world. He yearns for his Amish roots, but his past mistakes keep him from returning home.

Mary Lou is recovering from a medical scare. Her journey has impressed upon her how precious life is, so she decides to go on rumspringa to see the world.

While in the city, Mary Lou meets Jonah. Unable to understand his foul attitude, especially towards her, she makes every effort to share her faith with him. As she helps him heal from his past, an attraction develops.

Will Jonah's heart soften towards Mary Lou? What will God do with these two broken people?

Elijah: An Amish Story Of Crime And Romance

He's Amish. She's not. Each is looking for a change. What happens when God brings them together?

Elijah Troyer is eighteen years old when he decides to go on a delayed Rumspringa, an Amish tradition when adolescents venture out into the world to decide whether they want to continue their life in the Amish culture or leave for the ways of the world. He has only been in the city for a month when his life suddenly takes a strange twist.

Eve Campbell is a young woman in trouble with crime lords, and they will do anything to stop her from talking. After a chance encounter, Elijah is drawn into Eve's world at the same time she is drawn into his heart. He is determined to help Eve escape from the grips of her past, but his Amish upbringing has not prepared him for the dangers he encounters as he tries to pull Eve from her chaotic world and into his peaceful one.

Will Elijah choose to return to the safety of his family, or will the ways of the world sink their hooks into him? Do Elijah and Eve have a chance at a future together? Find out in this action-packed standalone novel.

Songbird Cottage Beginnings (Pleasant Bay Prequel)

Available for FREE on Amazon

Set on Canada's picturesque Cape Breton Island, this book is perfect for those who enjoy new beginnings and countryside landscapes.

Sam MacAuley and his wife Annalize are total opposites. When Sam wants to leave city life in Halifax to get a plot of land on Cape Breton Island, where he grew up, his wife wants nothing to do with his plans and opts to move herself and their three boys back to her home country of South Africa.

As Sam settles into a new life on his own, his friend Lachlan encourages him to get back into the dating scene. Although he meets plenty of women, he longs to find the one with whom he wants to share the rest of his life. Will Sam ever meet "the one"?

Get to know Sam and discover the origins of the Songbird Cottage. This is the prequel to the rest of the Pleasant Bay series.

The Crystal Crescent Inn Boxed Set (Sambro Lighthouse Complete Series)

Amazon bestselling author Sylvia Price's Sambro Lighthouse Series, set on Canada's picturesque Crystal Crescent Beach, is a feel-good read perfect for fans of second chances with a bit of history and mystery all rolled into one. Enjoy all five sweet romance books in one collection for the first time!

Liz Beckett is grief-stricken when her beloved husband of thirty-five years dies after a long battle with cancer. Her daughter and best friend insist she needs a project to keep her occupied. Liz decides to share the beauty of Crystal Crescent Beach with those who visit the beautiful east coast of Nova Scotia and prepares to embark on the adventure of her life. She moves into the converted art studio at the bottom of her garden and turns the old family home into The Crystal Crescent Inn.

One of her first visitors is famous archeologist, Merc MacGill, and he's not there to admire the view. The handsome bachelor believes there's an undiscovered eighteenth-century farmstead hidden inside the creeks and coves of Crystal Crescent, and Liz wants to help him find it.

But it's not all smooth sailing at the inn that overlooks the historic Sambro Lighthouse. No one has realized it yet, but the lives of everyone in Liz's family are intertwined with those first settlers who landed in Nova Scotia over two hundred and fifty years ago. Will they be able to unravel the mystery? Will the lives of Liz's two children be changed forever if they discover the link between the lighthouse and their old home?

Take a trip to Crystal Crescent Beach and join Liz, her family, and guests as they navigate the storms and calm waters of life and love under the watchful eye of the lighthouse and its secret.

About the Author

SP

Sylvia Price

Now an Amazon bestselling author, Sylvia Price is an author of Amish and contemporary romance and women's fiction. She especially loves writing uplifting stories about second chances!

Sylvia was inspired to write about the Amish as a result of the enduring legacy of Mennonite missionaries in her life. While living with them for three weeks, they got her a library card and encouraged her to start reading to cope with the loss of television and radio, giving Sylvia a newfound appreciation for books.

Although raised in the cosmopolitan city of

Montréal, Sylvia spent her adolescent and young adult years in Nova Scotia, and the beautiful countryside landscapes and ocean views serve as the backdrop to her contemporary novels.

After meeting and falling in love with an American while living abroad, Sylvia now resides in the US. She spends her days writing, hoping to inspire the next generation to read more stories. When she's not writing, Sylvia stays busy making sure her three young children are alive and well-fed.

Subscribe to Sylvia's newsletter at newsletter.sylviaprice.com to stay in the loop about new releases, freebies, promos, and more. As a thank-you, you will receive several FREE exclusive short stories that aren't available for purchase!

Learn more about Sylvia at amazon.com/author/sylviaprice and goodreads.com/sylviapriceauthor.

Follow Sylvia on Facebook at facebook.com/sylviapriceauthor for updates.

Join Sylvia's Advanced Reader Copies (ARC) team at arcteam.sylviaprice.com to get her books for free before they are released in exchange for honest reviews.

Made in the USA
Columbia, SC
11 November 2024

46207353R00119